BOYS OF BABYLON

CRAIG RORY DRAHEIM

BOYS
OF
BABYLON

BOYS OF BABYLON

CRAIG RORY DRAHEIM

ARPress
ILLUMINATING IDEAS,
EMPOWERING VOICES

ARPress
45 Dan Road Suite 5
Canton MA 02021

Hotline: 1(800) 220-7660
Fax: 1(855) 752-6001

Ordering Information:
Quantity sales. Special discounts are available on quantity purchases by corporations, associations, and others. For details, contact the publisher at the address above.

Printed in the United States of America.

ISBN-13:   Paperback   979-8-89389-737-1
               eBook   979-8-89389-738-8

Library of Congress Control Number: 2024922071

Table of Contents

Chapter 1 1

Chapter 2 19

Chapter 3 37

Chapter 4 44

Chapter 5 54

Chapter 6 63

Chapter 7 70

Chapter 8 80

Chapter 9 90

Chapter 10 102

Chapter 11 114

Chapter 12 128

"And he showed me a pure river of water of life, clear as crystal, proceeding out of the throne of God and of the Lamb."

– REVELATION 22:1

CHAPTER 1

Down by the river with sloping, sandy banks, topped with pines and cedars, Aqua should have known that if Sup was already in the water with the others, that they were ready to go ahead with the plan. *Plan*—the word made Aqua nauseated. Even though he did want to stall, Aqua genuinely thought he had enough time to piss, and that everyone would wait for him. So, it came as a surprise when he heard the commotion of his friends wrestling the boy under the water, only giving the kid enough time to plead, "Hey, hey," before he was murdered. Or rather, before *it was his time.*

It wasn't a plea in his tone, really. It was shocked confusion, like all the others. He never suspected that those would be his last words. Even in the final residual moment, after all the thrashing about, trying to find air, and while the mind could still process thought; even just before the darkness, the boy probably questioned if it was a joke or initiation. The crucial seconds of his life that remained were not wasted on the memories of his parents or dog, or the girl who sat next to him in school because she wanted to, but confusion. Aqua's friends had tricked the boy by telling him where he could find hundreds of Petoskey and pudding stones (even though the kid didn't know what they were) on the river bottom, and he trusted them as if they'd always been friends. The boy had wandered away from his family's campsite to explore, running into Aqua and the others while they were hanging out near one of their many tree forts. Aqua became fond of the boy in the few short hours he knew him, the two of them talking excitedly about superheroes and their nemeses. The kid liked comics too and, apparently, had quite a collection of DC Comics at his home in Akron, Ohio. Plus, "Mint Batman issues from the 1960s," that were given to him by his "favorite uncle." Aqua thought at least Moe would share in that fondness, and not because of the comics, but because Moe usually liked everyone Aqua did. It seemed as though this boy could be an exception, and Aqua was trying to think of a way to tell Supper this, but without sounding soft. And then maybe the boy could hang out with them until his family had to go back to Akron. After that, they'd be free to make a plan for someone else, someone they hated, like the first boy they'd drowned. Well, rather, the first boy Supper drowned.

The sound of the unexpected splashes caused Aqua to jerk, catching his penis in his zipper as he darted a look over his shoulder and saw a glimpse of that wild, disbelieving stare in the boy's profile. With his scrotum firmly snared in the zipper, Aqua couldn't release it for fear of doing more damage, maybe ripping the skin. The pinch was extremely painful, but he didn't want the others to know, so he kept silent and clenched his teeth—like a hero in a movie, he told himself—enduring the wound, but nonetheless forging on to finish the mission. The last time he pinched his dick had been when he was seven years old. Now thirteen, and the only one in the group not experiencing some level of puberty, no voice change, pimples, or growth spurt, as the others kept pointing out to him. He knew the dick pinch could make him look that much more immature. But he and his friends had bigger things to worry about at the moment, such as making their getaway from the river that instant. Aqua dropped the bottom of his oversized sweatshirt down to cover his crotch, and then jumped on his bike like the other boys, keeping his feet on the pedals and crotch off the seat. It would take him too long to try to work the skin loose, and everyone had to hurry.

In an orderly line, like a team for the Tour de France, crouched as if to avoid wind resistance, they careened along the trail, between the evergreens and waist-high ferns, then back out onto the old railroad bed, which had long since had the steel and ties removed, making way for the overgrowth of patchy vegetation. It was the end of July, and the deer flies were still around, orbiting the boys' heads in retaliation after being disturbed from their resting spots in the weeds. Usually pretty competitive on his bike, Aqua was now bringing up the rear and agonizing at every push on the pedals, feeling as if the zipper was tearing the skin more and more with each movement. He was afraid to look down, and imagined he was leaving a trail of blood. *That would be the evidence that would convict them all, a trail of blood from his penis.* He longed for when they could turn off at Beaver Pond and into their secret hiding place among the birches and hemlocks. Sweat was beading on his tanned forehead, less from the exertion and heat, and more from the pain and panic. When the boys did finally reach their destination, Aqua dropped off his bike and curled in a fetal position among the dried leaves and pine needles, holding onto his crotch. He couldn't pretend any longer or hide it from his friends. He was afraid he had done irreparable damage. The thought of not being able to perform sex when the opportunity ever became available to him caused panic. He would never become a man now. Perhaps he deserved this for not trying to stop the killings sooner. God was finally punishing him, but why him and not the others as well? *But why would God punish him? Things happen for a reason, right?*

Sup, the first one other than Aqua to dismount his bike between the semicircle of smoothed white birches, turned and noticed his friend lying on the ground. "Hey, what's wrong with Aqua?" The other boys looked at their friend as if he'd been shot. No one answered as Sup sloshed over in his wet pants, and then knelt down. "Dude, what's wrong with you?" Aqua didn't want the others to hear, so he spoke softly. Sup leaned in closer so he could hear. The other boys drew in nearer as well. Sup turned and looked up into their faces with a serious expression, then he began to smile. "Aqua got his dick pinched in his zipper." All the boys started laughing, except Moe, but especially TJ. Moe still couldn't help sporting a grin, though he at least put his hand over his mouth, to hide it a bit.

"It's not funny!" Aqua shouted, both embarrassed and angry. Saying that only made the others laugh harder.

"He's right," Sup hissed, to quiet the group. Everyone looked around and over their shoulders.

* * * * *

Aqua and his friends were ordinary and predictable by most standards and were often getting into trouble for doing boy things—mesmerized by explosions and loud objects, laughing every time someone farted, and becoming nervous around pretty girls, then clumsily pulling pranks on them—but, in particular, they anticipated every summer vacation, and with the arrival of that season, they felt they had a bigger part in the grand scheme of things and were masters of their own destinies. They solved their own conspiracies, conquered their own challenges, and emerged triumphant under extraordinary odds.

The boys were all introduced to each other in preschool, held in the basement of a local Transfiguration Church, in a small town, and one of the boys also happened to be the son of the attending minister. Despite the name tags they wore that first day, they each had to stand up in front of the class and tell the others their name, since none of them could read what the name tags said at the time. The town they lived in was distinguished with two main rivers, many creeks, and put on the map because of two large lakes bordering its east and west boundaries. This was land once fished, trapped, and hunted by the Algonquian family tribes (Chippewa, Ottawa, Ojibwe, etc.). A century and a half earlier, copper mining, logging companies, and other opportunists seeking the American dream bought, bartered, swindled, burned, and stole much of the region. Left behind was a vacation, sporting, and recreational area for wealthy businessmen and their families out of Chicago, Columbus, Fort Wayne, and Detroit. The land revitalized during the Depression and then was mostly forgotten until the late nineteen seventies, when retirees and tourism introduced commerce again. For adventurous young boys, it was rich in conifers and sporadic deciduous trees grown in just the right places for climbing. Mainly, though, it was a land of evergreens. Poison ivy grew in areas closest to the water or along the old railroad bed that bordered the swamp, and among the raspberry bushes, but all the boys were immune to it and even relished it, because it kept many people away from their favorite areas. Blueberries grew mostly along the tree lines, parallel to dusty dirt roads that few noticed except for the boys, and in late June and early July, these made for little treats during their explorations, and for great stains in spitting battles as well. There was no public sewer system in town. Every house and business had their own septic tank and drain field, but not necessarily their own well. Some wells were artesian and communal, or point wells, while others were tapped ninety, to as high as three hundred, feet deep. The roads in town were named after the trees, and paved, but most were barely wide enough for two cars to pass each other without one riding the shoulder. The road crew kept them cobbled together with cold patch, so they were lumpy and uncomfortable to travel, which most of the residents liked because they worked as unintended speed bumps. Other than the main state roads, every thoroughfare outside of town was either gravel or a sandy two-track. Though much of the soil was poor for planting gardens, those who did have gardens became sport for the boys, so they didn't have to return home for lunch. Food was plentiful. During festivals the boys got all the free samples, weaving in and out of the crowds of visitors and townsfolk, getting handouts from parents or teachers donating their time, and even the dumpster behind a local restaurant occasionally made for a good snack, particularly if they knew the dishwasher was popping out the back for a cigarette break, and throwing stuff out simply because it was outdated. Not that any of the boys' families were poor, although Moe's mother periodically went to the food pantry at the Catholic Church in Lintzville. The town was close to being a cliché, a brushstroke by Norman Rockwell of a small town in the upper Midwest on the cusp of the Iraq and Afghan wars.

It was a land that attracted tourists, "fudgies" or "trolls," as the locals fondly called them when they spent money, or maliciously when they didn't. And then, of course, there were the sportsmen from downstate who came for sturgeon spearing in the winter; steelhead fishing, wild turkey hunts, and mushroom picking in the spring; color tours and duck hunting in the early fall; and in the late fall, deer season, Christmas for sportsmen. But in the summer months the population would fluctuate dramatically, turning it into a small and thriving metropolis, people looking to swim, boat, kayak, canoe, and tube in the cool, fresh waters. Aside from the chaos and sin of those three warm months, the town of devout Christians, whether attending the church where the boys went to preschool, or one of three other churches, enjoyed a sedate and uneventful existence. Although, there was the time when one of its own killed a transplanted real estate agent and developer, then set his house on fire, but that turned out to be a minor blemish on the town's history, as the developer wasn't considered a native of the area, and on top of that, he was merely Asian, seemingly surrealistic with his kinetic nature among Anglo-Saxon features and at an arm's length sociability. In fact, nearly everyone in town was unaware of his origin—Japanese, Korean, Chinese, no one knew or really cared.

They just knew he and his kind were buying up America. And then there was the occasional drowning due to inexperience, recklessness, and lack of stamina, but this was nobody's fault but their own.

The world was primarily made up of three townships for the boys. And there was probably little of it they hadn't walked to, ran to, swam to, jungle climbed on, crawled on, or rode their bikes to. To the boys, these were the townships of their wealth, luxury, and wickedness. This was their utopia and their Babylon. When the boys went into kindergarten, of course, they were enlisted into the same public school. Oddly, they all stayed close to one another through elementary school, and then into middle school, a time when, as a general rule, many friendships end, as children start to evolve into different groups, or be ardently coerced by their parents to stay away from some and gravitate toward others. These boys were definitely an exception to that rule. But, then again, their parents took comfort in the fact that they all attended the same church, thus assuming the other parents had the same "core values." And they did, except for Aqua's grandpa. However, he was harmless enough, old, and kept his views to himself. But as for the others, they voted a specific way, and if they believed otherwise, they repressed it in order to survive and get along. Though the other churches were all comparable, Minister Troman had a way of keeping his congregation close-knit. He would oversee most events and had a charismatic likeability that never made him appear imposing when calling on members to help in various functions.

The boys had their own distinct personalities—at least as far as their age and community would allow them to. Supper, or Sup for short, was the unofficial leader of the boys, and the most confrontational. Hardly two months went by at school that he didn't receive a detention slip or get sent to the principal's office, relative to an argument with a teacher or coach, often over the semantics of an assignment, when Supper would suggest that the adult wasn't very specific when they gave direction. And it was that defiance that others admired. He had a very critical mind but used it primarily for sport. Supper, or Gary Bunker, was the only child to a father who was a general surgeon at a regional hospital an hour away, but also had his own private practice in town. His mother was an AA member first, but a registered nurse, who had been part of the longest nurses' strike in US history, which contributed to her addiction. She ran the private practice most days of the week, but, because she wasn't a PA, couldn't sign off on any prescriptions, but they kept samples from drug reps that would be handed out if necessary, when Mr. Bunker was in the building. This kept their business slow for the most part, with typically elderly dedicated patients, or those with sprains, cuts, flu symptoms, etc. Supper was a redheaded and freckled-faced boy. He had spent most of his life on the heavy side, but in the two years prior to the killings, he slimmed down to be, as his mother put it, of "average height and build for a boy his age." He had been compared by the girls at school to a young David Caruso from *CSI Miami*, but with longer hair.

Aqua had yet to achieve any sign of puberty in that summer, a fact that lent him no end of torment. The other boys already had, or were currently suffering, growth spurts, voice malfunctions, and hair sprouting in regions of the body that everyone giggled about. Aqua wasn't the youngest in the group. In fact, his birthday landed in the middle of the five other boys. He was simply a "late bloomer," as his grandfather put it. But what added to his dismay, was the fact that he was still the shortest one out of all of them. He was, however, the best swimmer, and could hold his breath under water longer than any of his friends, but then, being nicknamed Aqua certainly gave him the incentive to try harder. Originally, he was given the nickname because of his early fascination with the Aquaman comics, when he was six, seven, and eight—at least, that's what his friends thought. His fascination continued to the present day, actually, he just made sure no one knew about a collection he kept hidden in his bedroom closet, a collection he made sure to put away when his friends came over. Well, other than Moe, but he didn't care for comics.

Arthur Baltruss was Aqua's real name. At five, his parents "deserted him." A regrettable remark his grandfather had made, which was intended mostly for the boy's father, when no one showed up one Thanksgiving would forever remain in Aqua's mind. His parents initially moved downstate to get settled in their careers under the condition that Aqua would only stay with his grandparents for a couple of years. However, his father fell in love with a graduate student at the college where he taught English Literature, and then moved to the girl's hometown of Scuppernong, North Carolina, where he ended up "teaching spelling to Southern redneck elementary students, as opposed to the northern rednecks, if he decided to move back up here," Grandpa claimed. Aqua's mother stayed downstate, suffering bouts of depression and repeated bad relationships. Although she attempted to bring Aqua to live with her, her dad urged her to let the boy stay where he was until she could pull her life together, or at the very least, until her doctor could determine which medication would better suit her, Prozac, Paxil, or Zoloft maybe. It had been over six years, and Aqua's mother still hadn't found a "good man," stability in her career, or the right dosage of antidepressants.

* * * * *

"No one feels bad, do they?"

All the boys shook their heads and issued a couple of mumbled "nos."

"Cool. Cuz if anyone feels bad about the killin', you're not gonna get any stronger. We had another successful kill, and as long as no one finds out it was deliberate, then God's blessing is with us. Right, TJ?"

TJ gave Supper an affirmative nod. All the boys were quiet for a moment as Supper looked around at each of his semi-soaked comrades to see if they had a response. "All right, then, time for another burn. Who brought the cigarettes?"

Aqua pulled a pack of Marlboros and a lighter out of the bag strapped to the back of his bike and handed them to Supper. "Who wants to be first?" No one answered, then Aqua raised his hand as though he were in a classroom. He thought it would be a good idea to be the first one this time, especially after the embarrassment of getting his penis caught in his fly.

"Why's Aqua getting burned? He didn't participate this time." TJ spoke bitterly and gave Aqua a challenging stare.

"Yeah, he didn't help out this time," Creeper chimed in.

"That's only because you guys started without me," Aqua retorted defiantly, but not as convincingly as he'd hoped.

Moe stepped over near Aqua to defend him. "It doesn't matter if Aqua actually had a hand in drowning the fudgie or not. He was there with us. He would've helped if he wasn't pissing."

"I think that's a bunch of crap too. Look at the time we drowned that college girl. Aqua said he lost his pocket knife, and went running back to get it." TJ persisted with his defamation, determined to keep Aqua out of the burning.

"I did lose my knife, and it was the one my grandpa gave me."

Aqua surprised himself at how sincere he sounded this time. He suddenly became aware that defending himself added authenticity to his lies, and it gave him a boost of confidence. And everyone knew the story about the knife. It really *had* been given to him by his grandfather during deer season a year and a half earlier. They had been set up in the blind, and a nine-point buck walked into their range thirty yards out. Aqua's grandpa initially didn't want to give up the shot to his grandson, but he'd hunted for many years and had taken his fair share of venison, so he decided it was only right to let his grandson take the shot. Aqua had steadied the forearm of the .30-30 on the windowsill.

Grandpa coached in whispers: "breathe and relax" adding the need to "squeeze slowly," and that "the shot should come as a surprise." And it did. The deer dropped less than fifty feet from where it was hit. The bullet went right through the top of the heart. Because Aqua shot it, his grandpa said he had to gut it too. He coached him through that as well, rolling the carcass so the belly and rear faced downhill, cutting out the penis and testicles first, then around the anus, then slicing up the outer skin to pull back the fur, and, finally, the wall of the stomach from the crotch to the sternum. To Aqua, it seemed the intestines and organs came out like water balloons filled with mud. Aqua was squeamish when he began—it seemed immoral, like a desecration. The deer's eyes were wide open, dark and consuming, as if it were still processing everything going on and wondering why the world was so cruel. The animal had a human quality in its stare, something of judgment and mercy. But the more he cut, the more methodical the task became. When they were finished, the deer dressed out at one hundred seventy-five pounds. Too large for Aqua and his grandfather to haul out of the woods on their own, so Aqua ran back to the house and called his friends. Together, they put it on a sled and dragged it out of the woods, with TJ doing the lion's share. At the opening day buck pole for that year, it took second place. Only beat out by a fudgie who dropped his on a hunting farm, bringing in a ten-point buck that dressed out at one hundred eighty-two pounds. Aqua's grandfather had been proud and had given the folding hunting knife that he hunted with all of his adult life to his grandson. It was oversized for a pocket knife, bulging in Aqua's pants unnaturally, but it proved useful for many of the boy's summertime adventures.

"Yeah, Aqua's right, dude," Moe asserted. "Besides, he helped with that guy and his kid, remember?"

Aqua certainly remembered but wished he didn't. The memory was unbearable. The guy's son was only seven years old, according to the news media. Aqua initially pulled the boy near the shore, while his friends took turns tugging and jumping on the father from a logjam. Secretly, Aqua was hoping the father would break free, but it was probably the way TJ locked his legs on one of the logs under water, and then wrapped his arms around the man's waist, that finally did him in. Aqua knew he had to stop the boy from screaming. He also knew he couldn't let his friends and himself get in trouble. As much as he didn't like to see the boy's father taken from him, even though he was a fudgie, he loved and cared for his friends all the more. So as hard as it was, he knew there had to be a reason God was allowing him and his friends to kill. It all seemed senseless, almost like the buck pole. All those deer hanging in the middle of town on opening day. But they were going to be processed, eventually, into venison burgers, sausage, steaks, and the heads hung as trophies over fireplaces so boisterous men could talk about the hunt. "Is this what we are supposed to do some day?" Aqua thought. "Remember our great drownings?"

Aqua had to wrap his arms and legs around the boy because of his life jacket, floating and holding the boy under him until he stopped moving. The little boy's hands clawed back over his shoulders, breaking the surface of the water and, in a flash, exposing bitten fingernails. These indelible images stayed with him, as Aqua wondered if the boy bit his nails because he was nervous—like Aqua himself did. Or at least that's what Aqua's grandpa had told him, that he bit his nails because of nerves. And Aqua couldn't remember a time when he didn't bite his nails, so he had probably chewed his nails when he was as young as the boy he drowned.

Supper, fortunately, was smart and quick enough to take the little boy's life jacket off, so when someone found the bodies, they would think the father neglected to make his son safe, and that is exactly how the local news reported it. Channel Seven Action News also mentioned the rarity of having so many of the same type of accidents, in the same area, and in one tourist season, but then they attributed that to having such a record tourist season, lots of rain and high flood waters.

"All right, we'll vote on it," Supper commanded. "Everyone who thinks Aqua should be part of the burning, raise their hand." Gazing at TJ, Supper raised his hand, along with Aqua and Moe. Ry started to raise his hand, but quickly pulled it down after looking around the group.

TJ protested, unable to make eye contact with Supper. "Wait a minute, Aqua shouldn't be able to vote."

"That's stupid. Why can't Aqua vote?" Moe challenged bitterly.

TJ stepped over and squared himself up in front of Moe as if to try to intimidate him, but Moe didn't seem to feel in the least bit threatened.

"Because the vote is about him, and don't be stupid."

"All right, dudes, we'll just have another vote to see if Aqua should be able to vote. Okay?" Ry interrupted, after jumping over by his two friends. No one spoke, so Ry continued. "All those in favor of Aqua being permitted to vote, raise their hands." Supper, Moe, and Aqua all raised their hands again, and, again, Ry appeared confused on whether to raise his hand or not.

Creeper, now frustrated, pleaded to Supper. "Come on, Sup. You're not gonna let Aqua vote on this, are you?" TJ rolled his eyes, grunted, clenched his fists, and threw his head back in frustration. Before Supper could respond, Ry made another sincere suggestion.

"I know! Let's have a vote on whether Aqua has the right to vote on the right to vote or not." For a moment, everyone stared at Ry in complete disbelief. "What?"

"All right, this is crazy," Supper announced. "We're all in this together, and we stick together no matter what. The way we always have. The next plan we come up with, we'll just make sure Aqua takes the lead. Okay?" Supper looked around at each of his friends to ensure that they agreed with his reasoning. Ry and Moe responded favorably, while TJ and Creeper both reluctantly agreed in a barely audible 'yeah' and 'okay.'

Supper's defense seemed odd to Aqua. If Supper would side with anyone, Aqua would have sworn it would've been TJ. He almost always sided with TJ in some way. Aqua tried to read him, tried to pick up on anything in his facial expression or a telling glance his way, but nothing was there. Supper appeared all business and unattached. Then again,

Supper was always the diplomatic one in the group it seemed, normally settling squabbles or bad feelings.

Aqua turned around with his back to the other boys and lifted up his shirt to his shoulders, keeping his arms above his head. Two of the other boys stood on either side of Aqua, grabbing his arms tight, and getting a grip on his waistband with their other hand. Supper lit up a cigarette, taking a few puffs to get a good red-hot tip on the end. He squinted and blinked his eyes from the smoke irritation, then burrowed the cigarette under Aqua's left shoulder blade without any hesitation, in a horizontal line below three other scars that looked as though they had been made the same way. Aqua winced and groaned, and after Supper pulled the cigarette away, he let out a sigh of relief. "Next," Supper commanded, as if the boys had been drafted into the Army and they were all going through a line to get shots for a physical.

* * * * *

Though he looked more apprehensive than the other boys, TJ stepped up to be next. Terrence Jacob, nicknamed TJ by his parents, was often referred to as Supper's big, younger brother, because he too was a redhead, and to a great degree, looked to Supper as an older brother. Since preschool, he had been the tallest in the group, and it looked as though that would continue well into adulthood. He was the most powerful in the group, and yet had the least self-esteem. Being raised as an only child in a devoutly religious household, as his father was the church minister, TJ found Supper's rebellious nature and constant reassurance for the things his parents would consider vain or sinful, to be tantalizing. Although TJ was required to be home and ready when it came to church services or functions, his parents kept him off the leash pretty much the rest of the time, not really wanting him to interfere with all other aspects of their life, letting God babysit him for the most part. Other ways they kept him subdued was to diminish his achievements, telling him God only allowed him to do what he thought he deserved. And when TJ did poorly at something, that certainly meant God was disappointed. TJ made only a slight groaning hum when Supper burned him, but when he squeezed his eyes shut tight, a teardrop budded from each one.

"Next."

Ry hopped up for his turn, rubbing his hands together, then flailing his arms back and forth, exaggerating as if he were warming up for an Olympic swimming event. "All right, dudes, I'm ready." Ry was skinny and wiry, hyper at times and easily distracted. Supper had barely placed the tip of the cigarette on him when Ry jerked away. Aqua and TJ, who were holding on to him, grabbed tighter. Supper grabbed his waistband as well, to help keep him from moving. "Ahh!" Ry almost shouted but stifled himself. When the other boys let go, Ry jumped up and down. "God, I can't get used to that. It burns, it burns, it burns. Fuck, it burns."

Ry was short for Ryan Devos. None of the other five boys had called him Ryan since preschool. His crooked teeth and overbite made him the brunt of ridicule early on in school, but that was before his friends found out what was happening. Sometimes Ry appeared to be an insightful boy, recognizing the obvious, then, other times, he seemed completely without common sense, like the time he painted his hair green for a soccer game because all the other kids said they were going to do the same. However, Ryan didn't know that the other kids were using washable hair paint, and instead used a can of exterior enamel spray. He ended up making himself dizzy because of the fumes, not to mention the burning and irritation of his scalp that was so bad, he was immediately taken out of the game. He was shaved and treated for skin irritation after being taken to the Bunkers' clinic. Then there was the time he took a ski jump after only his second time on skis and broke his right arm. After seeing how far he flew into the air, everyone was surprised that he didn't break more, or that he even survived.

A few years earlier, Ryan had taken over his older stepbrother's bedroom after he joined the Marines. Before his brother left for boot camp, he warned Ryan that the room would take some getting used to, but wouldn't tell him why. The first night he slept in it, he knew right away. Being directly below his parents' bedroom, Ryan learned that his parents had a very active sex life. Soon Ryan got into the habit of going to bed with headphones and built on to his brother's already extensive CD collection he had left behind for him. The stereo was also left by his brother, along with a wink, just before he checked in his bags at the Cherry Capital Airport, before being flown to Detroit, and then on to Paris Island. "The stereo's yours now, little dude. Trust me when I tell you that you'll get plenty of use out of it." And Ryan did, not just to drown out the constant thudding and his stepmother's moans, but he actually wanted to hear the music that his brother liked to play, as a kind of homage in his memory. Three months after he was out of boot camp, Ryan's brother was training in Twentynine Palms, California, when a Humvee backed over his shelter-half while he was asleep, having just come off watch, and the rear tire crushed his skull and snapped his neck. Ryan was amazed to find that his parents had no change in their routine, resuming their nighttime activities just a few short days following his brother's funeral. He assumed it was the way adults dealt with grief and left it at that.

Ry loved his friends more than he loved his family. And if there was ever any division in the group, he tried tirelessly to mend the conflict. But he also had a habit of glossing over realities that he had no control over.

Before Supper could say "next," Moe stepped up to be burned, but he had to wait until another cigarette was lit. The other one had become impossible to use. Moe's real name was James Moby. The other boys called him Moe until the *Lord of the Rings* movies came out. Then, for a small period, everyone called him Frodo. Looking like the tanned version of Frodo, complete with the same hairstyle, there wasn't much Moe could do when his friends couldn't help themselves from doing parodies of the trilogy in ethnic stereotypes, such as hip-hop rhymes, where Supper pretended to be Gandalf. Outside the group of boys, other kids thought the "Moe" came from an abbreviation of Moby. It actually came from the time TJ's parents called the boy mulatto, and TJ didn't know what it meant or how to correctly pronounce it and went to school telling his friend that Moe was mo-latto, as if he were the descendent of a lost civilization. "Mo" morphed into "Moe" because of the *Three Stooges*. In the past year, Moe had been through a dramatic transformation after he hit puberty and had developed into a cross between a young Michael Jackson and Robbie Benson. This brought his previous nickname back, as the other one no longer applied. Especially with the added growth spurt.

Having sharp green eyes, brown curly hair, and dark skin, Moe was the only student of color in their school. There were some third and even fewer second-generation Native Americans, but the features that once identified their ancestors were now just subtle remnants. TJ's parents knew that he hung around with Moe and would often caution him to keep an eye on his friend, saying one day the black in him would come out and James could end up like his father, who was serving time downstate for armed robbery and drug trafficking, though neither was as dramatic as they sounded. He had held up tellers with a replica BB gun and was caught selling pot to his cousin and two friends. The latter charges the cops discovered after a warrant to search his apartment for the robberies.

Moe's mother, Karen, worked two jobs and had only dated once since she moved to the area, when her boy was only a toddler, and that relationship ended with only contempt and humiliation. After the locals found out about Moe's father, as the mother made the mistake of confiding in a coworker, she thought to be a friend, the single men mostly kept their distance. The men who did come near were leftovers that you find in a small town, sitting at the same stool day after day either at the bar or auto parts store. But it was hard to leave, and, besides, she had found a niche, someplace safe. And then she became used to it.

Karen joined the church where Moe ended up going to preschool and learned that the quickest way to assimilate in a small town was to praise Jesus. When Moe was around, most girls in the school would become catty toward one another, not just because of the mixed features that made him a beautiful boy, but also because of the potential image he could have, knowing his father was in jail. One thing puberty didn't give him was the sexual desire that it gave most other boys. If anything, it was his drive for music that became more and more intense. He played piano and was beginning to get a great deal of recognition from other school districts. He was compared to a young Oscar Peterson, because the middle school principal was aware of only a few black musicians and felt compelled to give the boy encouragement. He was only able to play on either the church or school pianos, because his mother couldn't afford to have one at home, nor did she have the space for one. Moe did, however, have a small electronic keyboard that he would practice with, laying it on his lap at nights while sitting up in his bed. Aqua was Moe's closest friend, both confiding to each other about things they couldn't tell the other boys. And Aqua, knowing how much Moe liked to play the piano, would invite him along the few times he went downstate to stay at his Aunt Liz's house for the weekend. She had a large grand piano and was pleased to see her nephew's friend putting it to good use. But that was the only thing she was please about. She commandeered the piano in a divorce settlement. It was one of the many things she got from a divorce settlement, and her ex was the only other person she knew of who could play it. To see the boy play, was poetic justice. Mostly the visits were boring stays filled with Aunt Liz talking about her trips and the people she met, and the pseudo adventures in which she climbed a mountain in Oregon, but turned out to be a foot path; went para sailing and made it seem as though she went sky diving; hit heavy turbulence in a plane and made it seem as like she braved the episode by looking death in the eye and saying she was ready to go. She was little different than Aqua's mother, self-centered and selfish. Only Aunt Liz took no medication. She was absolutely content in her own skin.

Moe was attracted to Aqua in ways he wasn't yet certain about. Aqua sensed it, or sensed something, and what he sensed, he liked. It made him feel unique at times, especially knowing that all the girls at school thought Moe was so handsome. Aqua never drew attention to it, because he was afraid that would spoil it. It was a secret he liked keeping. Moe had an effeminate quality that seemed more like the tenderness of a mature person. Often, to other boys and girls, it came across as a quiet confidence. But Moe was far less confident than he appeared. He started a journal in sixth grade, initially because Mrs. Grundhoff wanted everyone to. It was an assignment, but it was just to be about the highlights of their days and general observations. They were supposed to bring it to class and edit it for grammar and sentence structure. Moe soon started writing two journals, one for class and the other for himself. He found comfort in the latter, wrestling with his feelings and re-reading them. It was a way to tell Aqua and other boys how he really felt about them, hoping it would all make sense one day.

Moe let out half of an "Ahh" and opened his eyes wide as if the burn were a surprise. After he was let go, he let his shirt drop back down to his waist, while he continued to arch his back, not wanting the cloth to rub against the fresh wound. Just as Moe stepped away, Creeper filled in the spot to be the next of the group to be branded.

Jacob (Jake) Benjamin Arbuckle, aka Creeper, had been given his nickname by his sister, who was one year younger than him and commonly called him a creep. When she found him, role playing as a character named

Creeper in a Play Station game while his friends were over for his eighth birthday party, she prophetically announced: "Perfect, a Creeper for a creep." The name stuck. Creeper never could explain the connection, but he was somehow related to the silent screen legend, Roscoe "Fatty" Arbuckle. Something like the great-great nephew. But it didn't really matter, because none of his friends ever found this piece of news remarkable. The silent movies they did see, they thought were lame and low budget. Skipping several generations and all other branches, Creeper seemed to be the only bud on the family tree that showed potential of blossoming into the entertainment business. In fact, Creeper's family was so detached from the arts that, one evening at the dinner table, they contemplated writing a letter to Hollywood and asking why none of their favorite sitcom stars were nominated for an academy award. However, the family was very practical when it came to the rigors of everyday life and kept a regimented household, preferring the children to remain out of the house as much as possible during the day. To hear him tell it, Creeper was destined to become a great magician. Creeper also had faced blindness, which was off-putting at first, but gave him an uncanny ability to recognize details about his friends that others didn't. He was slightly less than portly, with full cheeks. His deep-set dark eyes often made him appear unemotional, except when he found something humorous, then his laughter was infectious.

There were some simple tricks he had mastered before leaving elementary school, such as finding a quarter behind someone's ear or cutting a rope in two, tying it, pulling it with a snap, then making it appear as a single piece of rope again. Eventually, though, he wanted to master escapes, like Houdini, but so far, any attempts had only caused him humiliation.

One summer when the boys were eight and nine Creeper went missing for two days, but on the first day, the assumption was, that he was staying at Aqua's house. But the second day after realizing there were no sleep overs or camp out among the boys, Creeper's mother and father reached out to the parents of all of Creeper's friends, then, with no clues about where their son could be, they had contacted the state police in a panic. When the police showed up on the second day to follow up on some more information, the trooper who had filed the report noticed the family's golden retriever scratching at the side door to a pole barn that sat on the property. It was used mostly for storage. Once he stepped inside the humid barn, the trooper picked up on a strong odor of feces, while the dog bolted over to an antique chest. Opening the chest, the sergeant found Creeper bound in cuffs both on his hands and feet, which were crisscrossed the exact way he had instructed Ry to do it. Ry had suddenly remembered something he had to take care of at home while Creeper was getting ready to perform the escape. He said he'd be back in an hour to check and make sure nothing went wrong, but Ry, absentminded as always, forgot. When Creeper's parents later called Ry's parents to see if the boy might know where their son was at, Ry's parents, finding their son in his room, assumed he'd been there all night. They had been role playing in their bedroom, and didn't appreciate the interruption, either. So, they were a little too eager to end the call.

Creeper had it planned that all he had to do was pull the key to the cuffs out of his sock, which was one of the reasons he wanted his feet and hands bound close together. However, the key fell from his grip, and didn't land on the chest bottom, but instead, slid through a crack in its slatted base. Being in a curled position, on his side, in a trunk that was no bigger than the frame his contorted body allowed, Creeper found it impossible to maneuver in a manner that would allow him to lift or budge the lid open. The humidity from the pole barn exhausted him into passing out at times, and the length of the chest, not to mention the length of his confinement, left him no choice but to defecate in his pants. He approached his stunts more cautiously after that, and certainly didn't rely on Ry as the only witness.

CHAPTER 2

Sup handed Aqua the cigarette. "Here, Aqua, you do me." He pulled up his shirt and turned his back toward Aqua. This would be Supper's fifth burn. He had one more scar than the rest of the boys. Although they had all been there at the first killing, Sup was the only one who had been physically involved in the murder. It happened the same week school let out for the year.

The six boys sneaked into a private campground on the East Lake, as they had done many times before. Besides the river, it was the best swimming hole in the three townships. There was a group of families from downstate staying at the twin lodges near the campground, and they had access to the same beach. There was a handful of boys, mostly cousins to one another, who belonged to the families. These boys were all in high school, just barely freshmen. While they stayed in the small town, they posed and postured in front of the local kids as if they grew up on *8 Mile* and were members of a gang. The reality was that they came from Bloomfield Hills and Farmington Hills, upscale suburbs outside of Detroit, which had gated communities or communities that paid for security companies to patrol their streets frequently and charge across the groomed lawns with tasers drawn at the oddest noise or suspicions of residents. They were all at least two years older than Sup, Aqua, TJ, Ry, Moe, and Creeper, swaggering with an air of authority that being promoted to high school gave them.

Supper noticed them before the others, as everyone else was too busy trying to dunk TJ. The friends were all in knee-deep water, squaring off with TJ, like in a movie, where, one-by-one, the strong main character deflected his attackers as they charged him. All the friends were laughing, and it was to the point where they all quit trying to actually tackle TJ, and instead, helped propel themselves so they would be flipped easier or pushed into the water more forcefully, as if they were rehearsing their moves to one day become stuntmen, among many other things they planned on becoming.

Before his friends knew that the boys from downstate were there, Supper was up on the beach talking to them. Aqua, standing and staring at the situation, eventually got the attention of the others. It seemed obvious to Aqua, just by the way the other boys stood, they wanted to make trouble, as they were either looking quickly back and forth at one another and covering a snicker with their hands or holding their heads back in a bold and threatening pose. The friends all walked out of the water to be near Supper. Once they were all away from the ruckus and splashing of the water, they, too, sensed that these other boys intended to make trouble. All except Ry, who immediately complimented the new kids on their "sweet Converse tennis shoes" and "Piston Jerseys."

The boy doing most of the talking to Supper addressed Ry's compliment. "Yeah, so which ones are your shoes?" the boy asked, looking down at the heap of shoes, clothes, and towels that the friends had thrown into a messy pile before jumping into the water.

"Mine are just the old white Nikes there," Ry replied, unassuming.

"You mean these?" He lifted a shoe up by the lace.

"Yeah, those are mine. They used to be my brother's. That's why they look so used. He still holds the best time for cross-country up at our school."

While Ry was talking, the boy started spinning the shoe around by the lace. Ry didn't mind because he always did the same, spinning the shoe around like a sling, then tossing it into the air to see how high he could fling it. The boy did the same but sailed it out into the water.

"Hey, that's my shoe." Ry ran back into the water to retrieve it.

As Supper was about to say something, while moving in closer to the ringleader, Aqua interrupted. "Why don't you guys just leave us alone? We're not bothering you." None of the boys from downstate replied. Instead, another one in the group picked up Moe's shoe and tossed it into the water, then, turning to the boy next to him, they cupped hands and bumped chests as if he'd just made a three-point shot. With that, Supper dove into the leader of the other boys, expecting his friends to join in the fight instantaneously, but the leader quickly knocked Supper to the ground and then pinned him on his stomach. Making it all too obvious that Sup was in over his head, three of the boys from downstate pulled out knives and collectively stepped toward the band of friends, while another rushed over and helped the leader hold Supper down.

"Get off me, you motherfuckers!" Supper shouted.

Horrified, TJ pleaded, "Let him go!"

"We'll let your boyfriend go if you hicks promise to stay off our beach," the leader demanded. Creeper and Aqua were about to agree at the same time, in order to protect their friend, but Supper spoke first.

"Fuck you, you fudgies." Supper spit with his face sideways in the sand as the one boy knelt down at his head, restraining his arms. "Go back downstate where you belong." The leader sitting in the middle of Supper's back pulled the cigarette from the other kid's mouth, and then burned the tip of it under Supper's shoulder blade.

"Ah!" Supper cried out.

Everyone except the boy who did it, seemed shocked.

"Now, you little pussies gonna go home and stay off our beach?"

Supper turned his face toward the sand to hide the tears. It wasn't the pain that made him cry, but rather the frustration, defeat, and humiliation. He knew his friends always looked up to him to take the lead in any challenge, and up until that point, in front of them, he always appeared victorious.

The six boys had never been put in a situation like this before. Never had they been threatened like this before, not with knives, and not by a group of other kids. This was a setback, a new and unfathomable experience. It was hard to process. Their senses were numbed, clouded—challenged in a way they were not yet prepared for. Occasionally, as has happened with all kids, they had run into a bully in school, but the bullies never took the taunting this far, and they had never been threatened as a whole. What could they do against the knives anyway? What could they do for Supper?

As the leader of the other boys backed away, Aqua expected Supper to be defiant in some way, to retaliate; maybe lunging at the other boy, or at least calling him a motherfucker, like he called anybody when he was really pissed. Instead, he got up slowly and kept his back toward his friends and his eyes from making contact with any of the downstate boys. Even when he retrieved his things, he tried to keep his face from being seen by his friends, by keeping a shoulder close to his cheek. Aqua followed Supper's lead in picking up to leave as the downstate boys all seemed to force themselves to laugh at their conquest. The rest of the six friends joined in, picking up their shoes, shirts, and towels, saying nothing and trailing in a crooked column behind their leader, Ry taking up the rear, but skipping now and again so he stayed close to the group.

TJ tried to get Supper to talk on the ride back home, peddling his bike up alongside on the gravel shoulder of the road, but Aqua could only hear mumbles, noticing Supper's blatant attempt to avoid him. The answers to TJ were abrupt, with a quick turn of the head, and were followed by Supper peddling faster each time TJ caught up with him.

The next day, Aqua didn't expect to see Supper, and he didn't, but he had a sense of how humiliated his friend must've felt and wanted to comfort him, even if only in some small way. His friends were the brothers Aqua never had. He knew they would never abandon him like his mother and father had. And although his grandparents easily filled in for his parents and loved him dearly, Aqua envied all the kids who had siblings, and how they must support and look after one another. By that idealistic reasoning, he wanted to let Supper know that everything was all right, a show of solidarity.

TJ called Aqua on the phone the same evening to ask if he thought Supper might be mad at them for not doing more. Mostly, TJ was worried that Supper was mad at him personally. TJ always worried about what Supper thought. The other boys got together, without Supper, down at the river like they always did, and talked about what had happened the day before.

They had several places along the river, for different occasions. One was at a logjam, where there was a sharp bend in the river. It was a good spot to retrieve belongings that the fudgies lost after flipping a canoe or kayak upriver. The strong current would push their things into a deep bottom, where large, jagged logs were intertwined and stuck in all directions, making the area look like a hazardous barricade against intruders. It was, however, one of the boys' favorite places to play. With vines interlaced on shore among the poplars and basswood, it made for natural swinging ropes and a Jungle Gym-like environment. The trick was knowing the current, as some areas could pull you under or directly into the staggered logs, but after years of coming to the same spot, and many dares, and many close calls, the boys knew the intricacies of the river and its current like a secret family recipe, where the ingredients were measurements of how many seconds to hold your breath, at what rock to start freestyling, what log to dive under, and which side of the river to be on for current shifts.

An area downriver from there was the boys' favorite swimming hole when they weren't up for any challenges—a deep horseshoe cove that was on the inside curve of the river. Like a pregnant belly that avoided the main course and current of the river, white cedars hung out over the hole at a slant. The boys had long ago cleared off enough limbs so they could climb out toward the tops and dive off into the water. Opposite the cove on the west side of the river was a small meadow on high ground. A large dead cedar had fallen from the east side and wedged itself in the V of twin poplars on the other side. The boys used this to cross over into the tall grass of the meadow, warming and drying themselves in the sun when the water would start to give them a chill, often in the same flattened grass where deer had lain moments or hours before them. And just when the boys became comfortable and settled, it seemed as though someone would be inspired by the clouds, or the tall, rocking weeds, to invent a game that would require the participation of all of them.

Another spot was six hundred feet farther downriver. This was where the boys usually met first, because it was closer to town and central to where they all lived. It was also a decent fishing hole, if you knew how to navigate the stumps and brush sticking out over the water's edge. All the boys knew how to cast their lines, but not without years of trial and error. Just about thirty yards into the woods on the east side of the river, the boys had cleared out a little area in the brush, where they dug a small pit for campfires, bordered with dried cedar logs and driftwood stumps taken from the water. There were also several five-gallon plastic buckets that they used for chairs, tables, carrying wood for the fire, or as a drum when someone got bored. They also built a lean-to out of crooked branches, with its back toward the water. This was just in case they got caught in the rain, but it was just big enough for all six boys if they sat shoulder to shoulder.

The days when they felt independent, they would bring frying pans and utensils, and then, use the fire pit to cook the fish they caught.

This was the place the five friends chose to meet without Supper. Moe was there before any of them, lying on his side under the lean-to. From head to toe, he was the width of the shelter. The pine needles made it comfortable, and the weather had been dry, so the sandy ground was soft and impressionable. Creeper was already at TJ's, and when Aqua stopped by, they all rode their bikes to the river together. It wasn't until an hour later that Ry showed up with his signature Pistons jersey on. It had been too large for him three years ago, when his brother bought it for him at a Piston-Celtics game in Detroit, and now the bottom of it barely draped over the waistline of his shorts.

"Hey, guys, so what's up?" Ry asked, as though he'd forgotten all about the day before, and they were getting together to go swimming or fishing.

"We were just talking about yesterday," Aqua answered pleasantly enough, knowing how carefree Ry was.

"Oh, you mean the thing with those fudgies from downstate?"

"No. We were talking about you flirting with Denise at the canoe rental," Moe interrupted caustically. Just before the boys had gone swimming the day before, they stopped at the canoe livery. One of boys' schoolmates, Denise Trindle, worked there in the summer because it was her family's shop. She also happened to be the most popular girl in their grade.

"Really?" Ry became even more excited, ready to talk about the girl he had more than a small crush on. "You know, I think she might have a thing for me." Ry studied Moe's expression for agreement, but quietly realized that his friend was being sarcastic. Without saying any more, he humbly walked over to a tree and leaned his bike against it, not wanting to lay it down in the dirt like the others because he had his towel strapped to the rack on the back, expecting, with his usual clueless optimism, that they might eventually take a dip.

Creeper, practicing splitting a deck of cards with one hand as he spoke, continued from where they left off before Ry rode up. "I don't know why that should bother Sup. I mean, those guys had knives and were older. There was nothing any of us could've done."

"Man, those guys were real assholes!" Moe blurted, staring at the ground and making lines in the dirt with his index finger.

"Yeah, but it's all over, and they'll probably be going home soon. I think we should just forget about it and stay away from the beach for a few more days." Creeper smiled after he spoke, but it had nothing to do with their conversation, but rather, the fact that he had finally managed to split the deck of cards.

"Well, I think we should do something to those pricks. Like pull a prank on them or something."

"I'm with Frodo," TJ added.

"TJ, please don't call me that anymore. I never even liked those movies as much as the rest of you guys," Moe complained.

"Okay, I'm with Moe."

"What if we get caught, did you think of that? No telling what those guys will do to us. I mean, they pulled knives on us for *no* reason. Imagine what they would do if we gave them something to be mad about." Aqua heard more concern in his own voice than he really felt. And it probably had to do more with the fact that Creeper's words seemed mature and rational. Aqua had also considered revenge, and even had some trouble the evening before trying to get to sleep because he imagined scenarios where he and his friends overcame the other boys, and then made them look foolish.

"That's easy for you and Creep to say because you didn't have a cigarette burned into your back," TJ challenged to the astonishment of the others.

Sitting Indian style on the ground, Creeper had just begun laying out a game of solitaire. Stopping, he cupped the remaining cards in his hands and squinted at TJ. "Well, if I did, I think one of the first things I would've done is tell my parents about it."

"Maybe Sup did tell his parents?" Ry found his friends looking at him like everyone always did when he asked a stupid question in class.

"You know Sup ain't gonna tell no one about what happened, partic-u-lar— partic-cu-larrr—mostly his folks." Moe started both impatiently and matter-of-factly at first but ended slightly embarrassed after getting hung up on particularly. "Besides, if he did, his old man would've called one of our parents by now, asking questions." Moe studied Creeper while the boys were silent for a moment. "Come on, Creep. Why ain't you up for a little prank? What about that time we chained Brent Misner's dad's fishing boat to the dock? That was your idea."

"Yeah, but he ended up breaking his arm, remember?"

"Well, it served him right. He stole your sister's bike, didn't he? And you sure didn't sound too heartbroken then." Moe was right. Even when they found out that Brent broke his arm, it had been a good feeling for all of them. They knew he deserved it. And it paid off, as the boys never had any trouble with Brent again.

A mischievous smile was beginning to make its way across Creeper's face, making it obvious he was thinking about some sort of enjoyment he got from the prank. He tucked his head down, pretending to look at the ground, but Moe and Aqua could still detect the smirk.

"Ah-ha! Yeah, I knew it. Come on, Creep, I can see you smiling there." Moe teased him lightheartedly now.

"All right, I'm in." Creeper lifted his head up with a full grin on and looked over at Aqua. "So, what do ya say, Aqua? You in too?"

Aqua wanted to make sure he saw Ry's expression before he answered. Although he knew Ry would go along with the majority, his unnatural silence during the discussion made Aqua feel he might have second thoughts. However, Ry was grinning along with the others. Then Aqua announced, "Yeah, I'm in too. I'll call Supper and let him know."

"That's all right. I'll call Sup and let him know the good news," TJ interrupted. Then, looking around at the others, he added, "Maybe we can all get together later and start coming up with a plan, if Sup's up to it? Whaddya think?" Everyone nodded in agreement.

Aqua felt a thrill of excitement, and it was comforting. Comforting because it was another adventure with his best friends, a secret they would swear to, like they did when they pulled the prank on Brent Misner. However, a sinking feeling replaced his joy when TJ called later that day and told him that Supper wasn't interested in pulling any pranks. TJ asked Aqua if he could talk to Sup. "I'll give it a try," Aqua replied. But he had reservations, because Supper had never been like this before. Maybe this was a time to just stay away and let Supper figure things out on his own. TJ then called the rest of the boys, and Moe and Creeper both called Aqua too, so that he might be persuaded even more to call Supper and coerce him into going along with the prank. Moe seemed so convincing in getting everyone else to come up with a prank in the first place, that Aqua suggested to him that he'd be a better candidate to call, but Moe insisted otherwise, remaining adamant that Aqua, of all the friends, was the only one who could convince Supper.

"Hey, Sup, how's it going?"

"All right."

"Me and the other guys were thinking about gettin' back at those assholes from downstate, and we were also thinking maybe you'd wanna help us come up with a plan. What do you think?" Aqua felt momentarily foolish for trying to sound spontaneous and original, as if TJ never called him, or that he didn't know he had.

"I don't know, Aqua. I've got some things I need to get done, ya know, and I don't know if I'll have any time for that."

If anybody in the group had free time, it was Supper. As his other friends were obligated to chores, or practices of some sort, but Supper had more freedom than anyone in the group, and Aqua was well aware of it. Hearing the melancholy tone of his friend's voice made Aqua want to come up with a prank all the more. It seemed like a further threat to him and everything he cared about that these other boys could put such a damper on his lifestyle, his surroundings, changing the things he was familiar with or accustomed to in one afternoon. "You know, we could probably come up with a real sweet plan if you could help us out, Sup."

"Ah . . . I don't know, dude. I'll think about it. Hey, I gotta go. I'll talk to you later."

"All right. Catch ya later, man."

Aqua relayed his attempt to the others. Never had he known all of his friends to be so bummed out at the same time. However, the following morning, Supper gave out the call to the gang to meet at the river, where they usually did their fishing, assuring everyone that he only wanted to hang out and really had no desire to come up with a "plan." As everyone showed up, it first appeared things would be awkward, like the time the boys tried to show their condolences after Ry's brother died. Before long, though, Supper returned to his old self. The boys watched an occasional canoeist go by and poked fun, calling out to them to "go home," or "that ain't the way to Detroit."

The day was warm enough early on with no wind, and as soon as the sun rose above the tree line, it became obvious the day would only be appreciated by the most serious of sunbathers having to only make minimal movement for the rest of the day, rotating the body occasionally for browning. The boys made their way upriver along the old railroad grade to the logjam. Forty feet above the level of the river rose a sandbank, where the boys would park their bikes and then jump like athletic contenders into the cushioned earth before entering the water. It was a guaranteed ritual. However, where the river went into the turn and the logs were pressed in the outside corner, the bank sloped back down to no greater than five feet above the water. In that corner too and continuing on for the next nine hundred feet or so, the wood became thick with cedars, hemlocks, spruces, tag alders, and three-foot-high ferns that made a cover and ceiling for another world of reptiles and small mammals. Aqua's grandfather had made the boys a breathing tube and attached it to a hose that they could be submersed under water and used while looking for treasures under the logjam. They ran the hose from the water, up the five-foot bank and along the ground under the ferns. At the end was a foam filter to keep insects or debris from getting in. At the water's end, Grandpa had fashioned a baffle and tee to keep the water from backing up into the tube, but that allowed the boys to exhale. The old man was not only on oxygen, but also had to take breathing treatments for emphysema. Using one of his circuits for nebulizer therapy, he was able to make the breathing harness for the boys. The boys made sure that no one else would be able to use it when they laid out the tube and hose, by burying the apparatus under sand and logs.

The top of the bank gave the boys an excellent opportunity to look for canoes, kayaks, and rafts coming from farther upriver without the riders seeing them. At times the boys liked to use the advantage to surprise and impress families, especially if they had young daughters in their group. The friends would run side by side, then, all together, jump through the air down the bank, yelling a war cry as if they intended to attack the unsuspecting tourists. But after they landed in the cushiony sand, they would only laugh, and then the families would realize that it was just a bunch of young local kids goofing off, though fathers, on occasion, had been heard calling them "little pricks," or "sons-a-bitches." What they knew about the rapid river and most tourists didn't, was that in the strongest area of current, as long as they didn't panic and simply allowed the river to move them along, they would quite shortly find themselves near a bank to grab a branch, or dragging on a sandbar, or steered into a logjam, where they'd be safe.

The boys dropped their bikes, scrapped their T-shirts, and prepared to jump in unison off the bank once again, but then heard the clumping of plastic kayaks coming from upriver. With nothing in view yet, they stood as close to the edge of the bank as they could and extended their necks like deer catching a scent in the breeze, jerking their heads from side to side to look over one another's shoulders. Their hopes were that it was another family they could have fun with, but it wasn't. It was a group of boys, or boys and girls, actually. Although there were no screams yet, something the fudgie girls could often be heard doing on the river.

"Are they older or younger kids?" TJ asked, with the implication that any of the friends who answered would use their own age as a barometer.

"Can't tell yet," Aqua replied. Ry was jumping around behind the group to try to get a better look. Noticing this, Supper chastised him.

"Ry, quit bouncing around. They can probably make out your movement through the branches." Supper gave Ry a stern look. The closest one was Creeper. As the kayaks drew near, he crouched close to the ground to get better sight, as one of the fallen trees from the bank's erosion was now in line with the boys' vision as the first rider was approaching. Creeper then spun around toward his friends, astonished.

"I don't believe it. It's those boys from the other day."

Everyone knew immediately whom Creeper was referring to, even Ry, who asked, "You mean the older boys from the beach?" to which Creeper nodded.

"Perfect, man. This is a good time to get the assholes back." Moe was instantly ready to wage war, but frantically pacing and chewing on his nails while he spoke, as if his steps would inspire a spontaneous and brilliant plan. "We can go down and make clay balls to throw at them."

"For what those guys did to Supper, I think we should do something worse than that." TJ made his announcement with the confidence that he had Supper to agree with him. However, Supper only stood quietly, shifting his eyes around at his friends, and looking occasionally down the river, as if timing the other boys' arrival. And as he did this, with Ry and Creeper joining in the chorus of trying to come up with a plan, Aqua studied Supper, but carefully, avoiding eye contact. Finally, just before it seemed like the varying ideas were going to turn into an argument, Supper interrupted.

"Hey, guys—hey! Guys, listen! I've got a plan." He pointed down the river toward the other boys. "It looks to me like the leader is the last one. By the time the other guys make it past the logjam and then around the second bend, we'll have their leader just where we want him, by himself. I'll go down to the logjam, take the hose, and wait for him in the water, behind the logs. As soon as I flip him, you guys run down and throw mud balls at him. We'll pelt him until he goes running home crying to his mommy. If we try getting all the guys at once, they'll probably only get out of their kayaks and try chasing us. This way, we can scare the pants off their leader, then we'll come up with another plan and get 'em all over by the beach. Whaddya think?"

Aqua was thrilled to see Supper taking part in the group again, and even appearing excited about it. He agreed, and then so did TJ. In an instant, all the boys were unified again and ready for their next adventure. Everyone took their positions on the bank, lying under the ferns as Supper circled down behind the logjam, easing into the small current-free pool between the staggered wall of timber and the shore, while hanging onto the hose so he could breathe when he was ready to submerge himself under and amongst the logs.

"Hey, you fuckers, wait up!" the leader shouted at his friends, who by now were all around the bend, past the logjam, and just going out of sight from Supper and the other boys. "Come on, guys, wait up!" The leader was the least steady in his plastic kayak. Just before rounding the next bend, the boy second to last took one last glance over his shoulder at his friend. He was laughing at the difficult time the leader was having. As soon as he was out of sight, Aqua led the charge down the bank to the muddy area, where he and his friends began slinging scoops of mud at the boy who had burned a cigarette onto Supper's back. The boy raised his arms and paddle out of the water to try to protect his face, but it unsteadied him all the more, so he crouched down for better balance. He shouted in protest, both with the intent to threaten his attackers and to be heard by his comrades downriver. "You mother fuckers!" But there was no way the boys in the other kayaks could have heard him, as they themselves were in the roar of the current, plus all the paddling they had to do themselves snuffed out the sounds of their leader. Besides, the rest were already around the next bend. There wasn't much time between the mud ball attack and when the kayak came upon the logjam, so focus and panic halted his cries.

To Aqua, the ambush seemed to go better than planned, with his own mud ball landing on the side of the boy's face. He felt like one of the patriots he was learning about in History class on the Revolutionary War, how they separated into small bands and attacked the British in unconventional ways, using the lay of the land to their advantage. He felt like David slaying Goliath with the same intensity as the pastor told the story in church. He was proud of himself and his friends and was thrilled to see them all excited.

The boy lost complete control of the kayak as it headed nose-first into the logs. The front rode up perpendicular onto lumber that was barely breaking the surface of the water but anchored at the front of the jam. With the nose now as a hinge point, the current quickly pushed the aft end ninety degrees, so the rear of the kayak was facing downriver toward the next immediate bend. Aqua noticed the boy seemed relieved for a moment that he hadn't tipped in the water, and as the kayak was now slowly inching its way downriver, though backward, the boy looked hopeful that he would soon be free from his attackers. But then Aqua saw Supper's hand reach up from under the kayak and grab the edge of the opening for the seat. An effortless tug capsized the unseasoned sailor. The other boys on the shore, including Aqua, cheered. They were vindicated.

The upper current swiftly pulled the unsinkable raft out of reach by the time the boy resurfaced, gasping for breath and struggling for a log to hang on to. Everyone cheered again as they watched the ringleader being jerked under water, but by the time he resurfaced the second time, panic had become obvious in the way his arms flailed and he gasped for air. Upon seeing this, Aqua became concerned and stopped applauding the victory. The boy looked, for an instant, like he wanted to shout something, maybe help, but there was too much water splashing in his face, and he seemed to be trying desperately to get air.

"That's it!" Moe shouted toward Supper, although he was still not visible. "Teach the fucker a lesson!"

Again, the boy surfaced, and again, he was pulled under, more desperate and terrified than the time before. Still Aqua looked at his friends, stupefied as they continued to cheer. Was he missing something? Did his friends know something that he didn't; that perhaps the boy really wasn't in jeopardy? The boy came up one more time, just barely to the surface, with his head tilted back in order to try to take in air, as if now he was anchored by weights and given only so much chain to work with, but it wasn't a second or two before he was yanked back under. Aqua could see him suck the water into his mouth. Was that it? Was the boy drowning now? How could he be? Moe, Ry, Creeper, and TJ were still cheering. Would they seriously be doing that if someone was drowning?

Only the boy's hands came to the top one last time, agitated quickly for something to grab, then disappeared from sight.

"Yeah!" the boys echoed in chorus as Supper came to the surface and climbed up on the logjam. Turning toward his friends, he put both fists in the air, claiming victory. Then, dropping his arms, he surveyed the water beneath him. But it was Creeper who spotted the boy first. "There he is!" Away from the logjam and heading toward the next bend down the river, the boy's body came just barely to the surface as it appeared to tumble and rock with the current, floating on its side at first, then rolling and twisting as it brushed alongside a stump, limp and useless. Supper looked over at everyone on shore.

"We gotta get out of here, guys." Supper spoke in between heavy breaths, as anyone would, being exhausted as he was, but everything about his movement and look showed a calculated urgency. Aqua was awestruck, but he knew, like his friends, to concentrate on a retreat. He also looked around to see if there may have been any witnesses perhaps coming down the river or walking along the riverbank.

It didn't occur to Aqua at the moment that he and his friends might possibly be able to save the boy. The way the body looked so useless floating down the river indicated to Aqua—and he assumed everyone else felt the same way—that the boy was dead for good. Dragging the body to shore and trying to resuscitate him might eventually get them all caught, and then how would they explain what happened? They were all there—they had all cheered. And then, what if the boy did come to life? Would he blame them for trying to kill him? Would they all be accused of attempted murder? Maybe the boy was only pretending? Aqua thought that could be a possibility. After all, Aqua himself did the same sort of thing quite often to tease his friends, and he was pretty sure he could hold his breath much longer than the boy had been held under.

Supper was the last one to get on his bike, after pushing it up through the ditch and onto the old railroad bed. Aqua glanced back in time and wasn't too far ahead to notice how cool Supper appeared as TJ hung back and frantically kept telling him to hurry. "Come on, Sup. We gotta get outta here."

Supper was the last one to roll in at the hideaway, less than a bike's length behind TJ. In the short bike ride from the river, everyone must have realized the seriousness of what happened, because Aqua noticed that the others looked as shocked as he was, possibly going over in their minds what would be the consequences of their actions. They all studied Supper as he dismounted his bike and carefully leaned it against a tree.

"What we gonna do, Sup?" Ry appeared more grounded than usual when he spoke.

"Whaddya mean?" Supper looked surprised by the question.

"I mean, that kid drowned because . . . well, I mean, he drowned because of us, and you . . . well, you . . ."

"What? Do you think I meant to drown him on purpose?"

"No. I'm not saying that. I'm just saying—"

"Wait a minute. That guy and his friends threatened us with knives," TJ interrupted defensively. "Remember what my dad, your pastor, always tells us, 'That everything always happens for a reason.' We were all just trying to pay back. What happened was an accident. That kid drowning was for a reason."

Did things like that really happen for a reason? Aqua thought. He knew the pastor said it quite often. Like the time the older brother of a girl they all went to school with, and who also attended their church, was killed when his snowmobile lost control and ran into a big oak tree. The pastor also said that God had a divine plan, and that it was the brother's time to go. Aqua imagined that the pastor would say the same about the drowned boy after hearing about it. Perhaps in the next Sunday service. The saying, and the fact that TJ brought it up, gave Aqua a certain comfort.

"Yeah, but we're sort of at fault," Creeper mentioned somewhat timidly.

"What," Aqua asked as a natural reflex?

"If we are, God will judge us." TJ cut Sup off, who looked as though he was about to speak. "And if it wasn't to happen, God wouldn't have let it happen. Sup couldn't kill anybody. It's not Sup's fault that the guy was a poor swimmer."

"I think TJ might be on to something," Moe added after a moment, when everyone seemed to be in contemplation. "Sup was just trying to scare the boy, weren't ya, Sup?"

"Well, ye-yeah, of course I was. If I thought he was drowning, I wouldn't have pulled on his legs, you know? Besides, the way you guys were cheering on shore, I thought everything was okay. But it's like the pastor always tells us, things happen for a reason, right? I didn't *want* to hurt the guy."

Aqua knew he had to mention what he was thinking, if just to get an explanation from his friends, in the hope that they could provide a justification. "Do you guys think that we should've stayed at the river and tried to pull the boy out?"

"My dad told me that most people who drown can't be revived, and that it's not like it is on TV, where they blow air into your mouth and you're automatically okay. Also, if we would've stayed and somebody saw us trying to bring the kid back to life, chances are, they would've found out what we did, and then the person would've thought we tried drowning him on purpose." Aqua stared at Sup for a moment as if waiting for a response, but instead, the response was answered by a couple of the other boys, who nodded their heads in agreement, and that was all that Supper seemed to need. Their nods made Aqua believe that they were thinking the same thing.

Aqua became less anxious about what Supper said. It was pretty much what he had thought as well. After that, there didn't seem to be any need to press the issue further. Aqua felt that any other questions would be hindsight, after the fact, and that wouldn't do any of them any good right now. He did, however, think to ask the others if they should call the cops, but if everyone else was thinking similar thoughts as he, then they had all probably considered the idea as well, and figured it was the wrong thing to do, since no one had said anything about it.

Aqua noticed a different quality about TJ as he stood in the center of the circle of boys and started to speak. "Tomorrow, at church, God will call us to judgment. And if he feels that what we did was wrong, then I'm sure he'll punish us. If not, it's completely out of our hands."

"That's right," Supper added, as if the suggestion had been his own. "I think we should all pray here together. If we are really wrong in what we did today, God will somehow tell our secret in church, and let everyone know."

Aqua found "secret" a strange thing to say. *Why did Sup call what just happened a "secret"?*

"I think we should probably get in a circle if we do this," Moe suggested.

The friends started to move toward each other, looking around at the others for direction.

"Yeah, good idea," said Sup.

"I think it would probably be better if we got down on our knees," Ry quickly added. But when he noticed everyone giving him a questioning gaze, he explained, "You know, to show more respect?"

It seemed logical to everyone, so they all settled on their knees in a circle, while, naturally, putting their palms together. "Wait," Ry interrupted. "I think we should hold hands to complete the circle. We're all in this together, and we should close the circle in prayer."

TJ nodded firmly. "That's right. That's a good idea."

So, they all clasped hands.

"Do you think that's the way your dad would do it?" Creeper asked TJ.

"Oh, yeah, I'm pretty sure."

All the boys were quiet for an awkwardly long moment, on their knees in a circle and holding hands, when Aqua broke the silence. "Who's going to say the prayer?"

"I think it should be Sup," Moe instantly replied.

"I think so too," TJ chimed in, with the others nodding.

Sup looked around the group. "All right." Taking a deep breath, he began: "Dear Father, please let us know tomorrow, at church, if what happened today was right or wrong."

Wait, what does Sup mean by 'right or wrong,'? Aqua wondered. I thought we were going to find out if this happened for a reason.

"Please let us know if what we done was wrong and let those in our church know that we done wrong, if we had. And, God, please watch over that poor boy that accidentally died today. And watch over my friends and me, because we are good people. Amen."

All except Aqua repeated the "amen." He simply mouthed the word, hoping that no one would notice. He was still puzzled. *Please let us know if what we done was wrong? God, I don't think I did anything wrong. Honestly, I wanted it to stop. I didn't cheer. Honestly, God.*

CHAPTER 3

Just the Sunday before, Pastor Troman said in his sermon that God can see into all hearts under his roof. Now Aqua became uneasy again with the anticipation of what the following day might bring. As soon as Aqua got home, he went to his room and opened the Bible his grandmother made him keep on the bookshelf on the wall by his bed. Aqua didn't know what he was looking for or where to start among all those ancient words, allegories, and chapters that didn't give much of a clue what they were about. He finally settled on Psalms, because that's what his grandmother always referred to. But even that didn't make much sense. " 'The Lord shall judge the people: judge me, O Lord, according to my righteousness, and according to mine integrity that is in me.' . . . What?" Aqua said aloud, completely confused. There was a quick rap on the bedroom door, and Aqua's grandfather poked his head in immediately after. Aqua barely had enough time to shut the Bible, with no time to hide it.

"Hey, dip shit, what ya up to?"

Aqua was lying prone on the floor, raised up on his elbows to read. He palmed the cover of the Bible to hide it from his grandfather. "Not much," he replied. With breathing labored and a slight unsteadiness, Grandpa clumsily stepped into the room and stood, bracing himself with the door handle.

"What's wrong? You didn't say hi to your old man when you came in." It was pretty routine that Aqua would sit and have a few words with his grandfather, usually right after school or after a long day playing away from the house, either to talk about his adventure for the day or ask his grandfather's opinion on something. Even if it was a hard question to ask,

Aqua would try to frame it in a way that wouldn't incriminate or implicate anyone. Aqua's grandfather seemed as though nothing could ever shock him. Even so, Aqua felt that this was too big of a problem—that he couldn't share this, even with his grandfather, like it was far too complicated, even to discuss in coded messages and third person references. Although it was largely skewed by the eyes of adolescence, Aqua was practically his grandfather's only connection to the outside world. Being housebound most of the time because of his emphysema and deteriorating lungs, and not wanting to join in his wife's church-related social activities, Grandpa would sit and mostly watch old westerns, play chess against himself, or tinker with electronics and old small appliances.

"Ah, nothin', just wanted to do some readin'."

"Since when did you take an interest in the Bible, kiddo?"

Aqua thought he'd hid the print on the cover fast enough and well enough that his grandfather couldn't see. "Oh, ah . . . I was just trying to look up the story about Noah. I was just thinking about it." Aqua forced himself to meet his grandfather's eyes and thought he saw suspicion.

"Ah, hmm." Grandpa studied his grandson for a moment. "Well, I can tell you, there's not much written in there about that old sailor. But if you're trying to find an answer to something, I can tell you right now, you're better off reading those comic books." Grandfather pointed to the ones Aqua had scattered on his bedroom floor. "The stories in that book were written too long ago. Everything's changed. The world has changed. That's only a rough outline. A first draft." Aqua nodded, his mind still partially clouded from what happened earlier, and puzzled by what his grandfather was saying. "Well, your old man has got to take his four o'clock neb treatment. I'll leave you alone to read about Noah, but if you really want to read a good sailing story, *Moby Dick* is a hell of a lot better."

"Okay, Pa," Aqua replied respectfully.

* * * * *

The last time Aqua remembered looking at his alarm clock, it registered 3:20 AM, then he heard his grandfather's crackly voice: "C'mon, Arthur. Get up and get some breakfast. Your grandma's makin' those pancakes you like." Aqua was able to focus just on time to see the old man's smile just before he shut the bedroom door. Then he looked over at his alarm clock. Now it was 8:32 AM. In an hour and a half, he would be at the church, along with his friends, awaiting their fate. His stomach was clenched so tight in nervousness that he was barely able to eat his favorite blueberry pancakes, and his grandparents asked him if he wasn't feeling well and double-checked with a touch to his forehead. When the examination showed no ailment, his grandfather pressed Aqua, asking if something else was bothering him, but Aqua thought it better to go with just complaining of a slightly upset stomach. However, when asked if he wanted to stay home, Aqua assured his grandparents that he would be fine, and also added something in regard to meeting with one of his friends, so as not to draw suspicion. Aqua also thought he might hear something at the breakfast table about the boy's death, but his grandparents seldom read the paper, and with the new cable hookup they had put in, they seldom watched the local news. If they had heard about the drowning, Aqua was positive that his grandfather would have already mentioned it and included a cautionary tale about playing at the river.

The boys sat in different spots around the church, as they always did, with their families. Aqua's grandparents always sat toward the back of the church, because his grandmother admired the minister a great deal and wanted to be one of the last people to file out after services, so she could chat with him longer than most. Aqua's grandfather found this to be annoying, but it was one of the few things he could do to make his wife happy, so he let it go.

Before going inside, the boys spoke little to each other on the church steps, except to ask each other if their families had heard anything about the boy, but no one had. Ry and his family were late, walking in just as Minister Troman told everyone where to open their hymn books for the first singing of "Praise to the Lord." But that wasn't where Aqua thought he and his friends would be given their intervention from God. Certainly, it had to be when the minister gave his sermon.

Minister Troman was a portly man with graying temples. He kept his hair in a crew cut with white walls. And having fat cheeks, it made the upper portion of his head look as if it had been pressed in a vise. With a short, stubby nose, even the small, frameless bifocals he wore would rest against his cheeks and raise when he smiled or spoke expressively, which is why he often removed them at the podium. Having inherited most of his mother's features, the only distinguishable trait that TJ received from his father was his droopy and bright hazel eyes.

"Today is a sad day for our community. As many of you are aware, and just like several others in our congregation, I am a volunteer member of our fire department." The pastor took a pause, while breathing heavily through his nostrils. "Yesterday afternoon a few of us in the department answered to an emergency call down at Stan Healy's property. His cabin on the river, not his home on the lake. Stan was approached by a group of young boys from downstate, who were vacationing with their parents. Apparently, the boys had been kayaking and lost sight of one of their friends."

Yes, yes. Aqua was sitting at the edge of his hard wooden pew. *Say it! What do you know?* Aqua thought to himself. *Call us out and get it over with already.* He began biting at his fingernails, a habit that had cropped up soon after Aqua's father left with the college grad to North Carolina— and one his grandmother had been trying hard to break. Noticing, his grandmother tugged on his arm. Aqua paid her little attention, instead gazing intently on the minister. Her wrath would mean nothing if everyone found out they had killed somebody.

"When the boys finally found their missing friend, the boy had drowned."

There was a collective gasp through the church, and Aqua heard his grandmother utter an "oh my."

"As a couple of the paramedics were giving CPR, I said a prayer with the other men who helped retrieve the child, but the good Lord decided that it was his time and sent his angels to take the boy's soul to heaven. God's will be done.

"As mere mortals, it's hard for us to understand God's reason, but he has a divine plan for all of us. It was that child's time. And as servants of the Lord, we must accept his actions and his will."

That was it? Aqua thought, his heart hammering in his chest. That was the message? *It was God's will that the boy be taken?* He looked around the church at his friends to see if the message was as clear to them. All except Ry, who sat staring at Minister Troman with his mouth ajar, made eye contact and gave a slight nod. Supper even wore a faint grin, and it made him look so confident that Aqua thought he may have known exactly what the minister was going to say. Aqua paid little attention to the rest of the sermon, except when the minister warned all the children to be careful when playing down at the river, because "many areas are unpredictable." But Aqua also thought that sounded a little odd, because if God had a plan for everything, why would it matter if you were careful or not?

The Sunday service ended with the choir singing "Shall We Gather at the River." Feeling a great deal of relief, Aqua's perception became more lighthearted, and he found the song to be an unexplainable irony, not related to him, but a sign from God . . . *maybe*.

* * * * *

"You heard what TJ's dad said. God has a plan. Obviously, we're part of that plan. If that boy died for a reason and we were involved, then what we did was right." Supper allowed a lengthy pause after answering Creeper's question, and Aqua could tell that everyone was giving it serious consideration.

It was another hot day, and the boys had retreated to Creeper's basement, which his father had turned into a rec room with a pool table, dartboard, and ping-pong table. It was cool and felt rewarding to the boys, especially because Creeper's mother kept the freezer under the steps filled with ice cream bars. There was also a television with a Play Station 2 that sat on a small stand between the couch and pool table. Moe and TJ were playing *Grand Theft Auto*, a game they all shared and kept hidden from their parents. When Supper began talking about God's plan, however, Moe and TJ put the game on pause. Aqua was sitting on the stairs to keep lookout, just in case Creeper's sister tried to spy on them.

"Yeah, dude, but do ya really wanna kill someone else?" Ry spoke without compassion but misunderstanding.

"All those fudgies and trolls are the same. They're not s'pose to be here. Look at the way they treat Moe's ma at the store." Everyone looked over at Moe when Supper mentioned his ma, and Moe appeared to reflect on what was said. Moe's mother was a cashier at a locally owned grocery store in town. Tourists would quite often express their discontent about the store's high prices toward the employees, whose hourly wage was a fraction of the typical customer's. In fact, most of the locals did their shopping elsewhere. People who lived in private associations around one of the lakes were generally even more rude and hostile toward the cashiers, feeling insulted if a clerk asked for an ID to cash a check and did not recognize their name as someone important, or if they accidentally bagged their groceries in paper bags and not plastic, unaware of what is more socially or ecologically proper.

For a brief moment Aqua was lucid, seeing where Supper was going and the enormity of what he was suggesting, and it didn't seem horrifying. It seemed exciting. Then he returned his attention to everyone else's response and what their feelings meant to him, particularly the one in the group he was closest to, and that was Moe.

"What'd your father say the other week, TJ? About how the fudgies come up from downstate with their bad ways or something?"

"He said they'd come up with their heathen ways. And that they don't care about our values." Repeating his father's words seemed to motivate TJ in siding with Supper.

"We have to stop these fudgies. If we don't, they'll just keep coming up here and ruining all our cool places. If we can teach 'em to fear the river and get on the news, then maybe they'll take their vacations somewhere else. We need to be strong. We need to make ourselves stronger than them."

"How we gonna do it, Sup?" Ry asked. But before Supper could answer, Creeper interjected.

"We're not going to just keep drowning them, are we? I mean, isn't that wrong?"

Supper looked astonished. "First off, that's how we'll get them to fear the river. And secondly, if it was wrong, God would've punished us already."

"Sup's right. What we did was God's work, and I think he wants us to continue it." TJ spoke with more certainty than Aqua remembered him ever doing before. Often, he was hesitant, or, if he interrupted with enthusiasm, he would apologize or look around to see if anyone was offended. Aqua suspected that Supper and TJ were speaking more to each other outside the group than usual, but they were, after all, like brothers.

Aqua thought of the terror in the boy's face just before he died. At the time, it seemed as though he deserved it. Especially after he had taken such pleasure in burning Supper's back. *Did God really use them to punish the boy?* Aqua thought about what his grandmother often said to him, and although the words echoed Mr. Troman's, they seemed original and more believable coming from her: "everything happens for a reason." And so, with what Supper was saying and the support he appeared to be gathering from the others, Aqua considered this decision to be something that was happening for a reason, like the time they pulled the prank on Brent Misner, and they were never caught or punished for that deed. Maybe he and his friends were guided and destined by God to carry out his wrath. After all, one of his friend's father was a minister. Oddly, Aqua felt, too, a conflicting sense of power. The secret he and his friends shared made them closer, more inseparable. It made them strong together. What they decided collectively had to be right.

Aqua looked up at the top of the stairwell, having caught a glimpse of light out of the corner of his eye. Creeper's sister was just beginning to ease her head through the opening. Aqua gave off the signal by clearing his throat in a big way. Everyone stopped talking, and after realizing she had been discovered, Becky marched down the stairs. Aqua stood up on the floor as Becky seemed to be coming straight down. But she stopped and put her hands on her hips just as she cleared the ceiling and could see everyone.

"Whaddya want, freak?" Creeper snapped.

"Mom wants me to ask you and your friends if you want some tacos?" Everyone looked at Creeper, then nodded or raised their eyebrows with an intended yes.

"I love tacos," Ry said enthusiastically. Then all the boys jumped up and ran up the steps past Becky. Aqua stood still and allowed everyone to file ahead of him. Becky looked at him oddly, then waved her hand for him to go ahead of her.

"That's all right. You go ahead." As Aqua was abreast of Becky, she looked at him. "You know, out of all my brother's friends, you're the only one I like." Becky then turned as soon as Aqua passed and marched back up the stairs, with some difficulty, taking two steps at a time, as if she were much bigger and more grown up than she really was.

CHAPTER 4

The six friends' next attempt at murder was a little better planned than the first killing, and all except Supper appeared apprehensive in making a selection on who they should target, watching canoeists and kayaks pass by along the river. They did, however, decide on some conditions or guidelines that would help ensure their anonymity. One was that they should attempt their crimes closer to dark, as there may be less of a chance of someone coming across the bodies so soon; or if the attempt failed in some way, dusk might make them less recognizable. Two was that they would set up a watch upriver, in case there may be someone else approaching. Three was that they were not to kill in the same area twice in a row, as that may draw attention to that spot, prompting someone to check on it periodically. And four was to try to take down only one person at a time.

A couple more days would come and go as the boys gathered at the east end of the river, at a point closely downriver from where many tourists were dropped off for recreation. Five college girls, enjoying the freedom of the summer, came floating down the river in inner tubes before dusk one day. They all appeared very bold to the boys and quite striking as well, with athletic bodies and two-piece bathing suits; lying with their butts in the hole of the inner tubes, they were tanning their legs, stomachs, and chests, or as best they could anyway. One had tied an additional inner tube to the one she was sitting in, and this one had a cooler wedged and tied in the center, filled with beer and ice. With the sun sinking, most parts of the river were cast in shadows by the trees lining the bank, and the banks themselves. The boys all listened to them for a while, as their playful screams ricocheted along the river's corridor.

Aqua didn't think at the time, and assumed the others felt the same way, that the girls would be an opportunity for them. Whenever they spoke of drowning someone, it was always in the context of another boy or a lone man. In fact, as the first two girls came floating by, hanging onto one another's tube ropes, Aqua's friends became quiet and were more focused on trying to find a better spot out from the trees so they could study the girls, as opposed to collaborating on a scheme to drown one of them. Even TJ, who became shell-shocked around girls, was looking for the perfect vantage point.

"Hi, boys!" a redhead with short hair shouted, and waved with her free hand, while hanging onto her friend's tube with the other. Aqua became suddenly curious about his friends' behavior. Ry seemed to be the only one kind enough to return the greeting with a wave and a "hi," however automated it appeared. The girls stretched themselves toward each other, whispered something, and then giggled. The surface current was slow off to the far side of the river because of its width, so the girls were able to grab hold of some hanging limbs and roots on the opposite bank and wait for the others without much effort.

"So, you boys live around here?" the other girl asked. She was less petite, and curvier than the redhead. And she was quite the contrast, with a deep tan and long, dark hair rolled into a tight bun.

Again, Ry was the one who hollered out an answer. "Yes."

Two of the other girls floated and hand-paddled themselves up to the others and moored their inner tubes together. They talked amongst themselves and appeared to be waiting for the last one in their party to catch up. Moe walked over to Aqua, who was sitting in his favorite shaded area next to a quad birch that he often warned his friends not to peel the bark off of, no matter how fun it was. One of the trunks was already beginning to die, where the bark had been stripped in stages up and down the body, making intermittent rings. "Hey, dude," Moe said, "those college chicks look pretty hot, don't you think?"

"Yeah," Aqua agreed, knowing it was the only right answer. To say anything else might make him sound childish, even to Moe, whom he usually felt he could be more honest with than any of the others. What Aqua really thought was that one of them looked too bony and pokey. Two others looked too mushy. Another one's face looked too wide, like

Mrs. Stankevich in the sixth grade, who always smelled like vinegar. And the last one, who came slowly spinning down the river, looked too bored to be any fun at all. In fact, even though all the girls kept glancing over at the boys and laughing about something or other they had said, none of them came across as though they'd be any fun to hang out with. Aqua knew that none of them could climb the way his friends did or jump off the banks like them. And they would probably make a real big deal out of it if they did try those things. Worse, they would probably complain about any challenge, like the older high school girls he noticed.

Once the girls were all together and holding onto one another's inner tubes, they appeared to be rapidly chatting about something with great interest, seemingly glancing at the boys in turns. Aqua noticed TJ working his way closer and closer to the edge of the bank and looking over the girls with an odd fixation. The girls must have noticed as well, as they started saying something to him that Aqua couldn't hear over the current of the river. Whatever it was caused TJ to find his way to the closest point on the shoreline from the girls.

The redheaded girl paddled her way out, closer toward the center of the current. Where she still had control of her inner tube with little effort, she pulled her top up to expose her breasts to TJ. He turned and ran back up the small bank and into the trees. As the other college students laughed, the girl pulled her top back down and shouted to Ry. "What's wrong with your friend? Hasn't he ever seen titties before?" Ry looked off into the direction TJ had disappeared in, then looked back at the girl with a smile.

"I don't think he has, but I don't mind."

The girl simply tossed her head back and laughed. This seemed to be a cue for all of them to shove off and let the current take them farther downstream, until they came upon a sandbar where they could get out of the inner tubes and walk around. Along the river, this portage seemed like some distance, but across land, it was only a short run for the boys, where they could spy on them from behind young evergreens and the summer ferns.

Aqua went off to look for TJ, but Supper was already much farther ahead of him, catching up with TJ shortly after he took off. Without them noticing, Aqua studied the two talking privately, Supper keeping his hand on TJ's shoulder the whole time. When the conversation was through, TJ trailed close behind Supper and met up with the others wearing a smile on his face as if he had been told there was a present waiting for him.

"All right, guys, here's the plan," Supper said with enthusiasm. "The girls are gonna come up on our diving hole in a little while. TJ's gonna wait behind the big cedar lying out across the water. If he hides under the bank, no one should be able to see him, but he should be able to see them. When one of the girls gets spaced out between the others, or gets separated from the others, I'll give him the signal from the other side of the river, where I'll hide in the ferns. Moe, you're gonna raise your fingers in the air from the next bend upriver and let me know how many are coming each time." Moe nodded. "If the conditions are right, Creeper will be waiting under the overhang and the inside bank upriver from TJ, where everyone always skirts by." Supper pointed at Creeper. "Then, all you have to do is go under the girl and poke her inner tube with Aqua's knife. You still got those swimming goggles, don't you?"

"Yeah, right here." Creeper pulled them out of his back pocket to show him.

"Cool. The girl will think she got punctured with a stick. By the time she gets down by TJ, he'll be able to pull her under. Just make sure you don't cover her mouth, TJ. I saw on CSI that if water don't enter the lungs, it won't look natural."

"Yeah, I think I saw the same one, dude," Ry was quick to add. "Because when someone drowns, they eventually suck in water."

"Aqua, let Creeper have your knife." Supper spoke without acknowledging Ry.

Aqua slapped his pockets in surprise. "I think I lost it."

"What?"

"It must've fell out of my pocket when I was running." Aqua wasn't sure he sounded convincing, so he kept his head down, as if looking around on the ground for the knife. In fact, Aqua had tossed the knife in the high weeds behind him as soon as Supper mentioned Creeper using it. When they were all just talking about it, planning a killing, it sounded exciting to Aqua, but now it was really happening. They were all going through with the plan, and even Moe showed no reservations. Aqua felt childish—his friends all seemed tougher than him, that they could follow through with something like this.

"That's all right. I'll just get a sharp stick to poke the tube with," Creeper suggested excitedly.

"Wait a minute," Ry blurted, fishing through his pockets. "I've got a knife." Ry exposed a small Swiss army knife. It was rusted, with the plastic red jacket chipped and cracked. He handed it to Supper, whom he was closest to, while Aqua still pretended to be looking feverishly for his own. Supper opened the main blade and studied it with a twisted look on his face. The point on the blade was rounded like a butter knife, and there was more rust than silver showing. Supper ran his thumb lightly along the cutting edge, keeping a distasteful expression. Then he ran the blade across his arm, pressing harder.

"Dude, this is the dullest knife I've ever seen."

"I sharpened it with a stone."

"A whetstone?"

"No, the stone was dry?"

"Not a wet stone. A whetstone."

"You're confusing me, Sup. What's the difference?"

Supper looked around at the others for support, but it was obvious he was confusing everyone else as well. "Never mind," Supper said, frustrated. "Creeper, just go ahead and find a sharp stick. Now, Aqua, I want— Where's Aqua?"

"I think he went to look for his knife," replied Moe.

"Okay, we'll just go on with the plan without him. It'll just make the rest of us that much stronger."

* * * * *

Aqua was reading the October 2003 issue of *Aquaman* when Ry called asking about cheat codes for two of the Play Station games, he had borrowed. The issue was "Deep Sea Dying." What Aqua found amazing was how he forgave Manta, a human with only simple mortal powers, but an earlier enemy. An earlier enemy who was the cause of the death of Aquaman's only son. Aqua weighed in on the allegorical message. *Jesus forgave too, and hurt nobody,* Aqua thought.

Within two minutes of hanging up with Ry, Supper called Aqua.

"Hello?"

"Aqua?"

"Yeah."

"This is Sup, dude." Aqua had thought Ry was calling him back and didn't recognize Supper's voice immediately.

"Yeah, what's up?"

"Everyone is gonna get together down at the Nigger Creek swim hole. Kin ya go?" This was a small creek that merged into the river, coming out of Crumley Swamp. Instead of adding sediment to the intersection, the converging water carved out a deep hole in the river. No one was sure how the creek got its local name, because it certainly wasn't named that way on any maps, but then, no one really questioned its origin. Aqua studied Moe's face several times when it was mentioned, but he always appeared unaffected, showing not even a grimace, flinch, or squint of the eyes.

"Sure. Do you want me to call anybody?"

"No, that's all right. I already called everyone," Supper answered in a quick burst.

Strange, Aqua thought. *Why didn't Ry say anything about the get-together when we were talking on the phone?* But then again, Aqua knew how forgetful Ry could be at times and assumed it would be silly to mention it to Supper. "Okay, dude, I'll be there in a little bit."

Aqua rode his bike down Brady Road, and, making sure there was no one watching from Mr. Norton's front porch, he crawled and pulled his bike under the electric fence and into the field where the grouchy old man let his horses run, then Aqua peddled as fast as he could the seven hundred feet to the other side, where he again crawled and carefully pulled his bike under the fence, being careful not to let his handlebars touch the wire. Less than a hundred feet from there was the wooden bridge Mr. Norton's father built in the thirties, so he could ride his horses over to the other side of the river, where there was a small orchard of apple trees. Beyond that were two rolling hills of hardwoods, which then sloped down into a cedar swamp that was divided by the river, and the spot that was the boys' favorite swimming hole. Other than Moe, Aqua's friends usually rode in from the other side, coming down the railroad bed, Aqua always found it thrilling trying to make it through Mr. Norton's property without getting caught.

At the swimming hole, Aqua found TJ sitting partially on a log just inside the high grass line. He was holding on to a cedar sapling so as not to fall back while pooping. "Hey, TJ, where's Sup and the others?"

"Oh, they're coming," TJ answered between grunts. He finished and pulled up his shorts.

Jokingly, Aqua asked, "Aren't you going to wipe your butt with some leaves or something?"

"It was a clean break. I don't have to," TJ replied contemptuously. He then walked over closer to the bank and sat down crossed-legged in a patch of dry moss opposite Aqua.

Two aluminum canoes came drifting in line down the river. There was a young couple in each one. They noticed Aqua and TJ and waved and said hi, but the two boys only stared at them, following their movement along the river as if they were a branch drifting by. The couples found it hard to keep eye contact with the boys and mumbled comments to one another, then nervously laughed at what they said. Unaffected, the boys continued to watch them until they glided out of sight.

"So, what's Sup got going on that he wanted all of us down here?"

"How the heck am I supposed to know? Ask him when he gets here," TJ answered impatiently.

The way TJ snapped and then wouldn't look toward Aqua, created an odd tension. Aqua knew that TJ had some random moments of moodiness, ever since elementary school, usually followed with a scowl and a glance in the direction of the person he was dissatisfied with, never appearing bellicose, more like he was hurt. TJ wasn't hurt this time. The tone of his voice was steady, bitter, and somehow accusatory. Aqua decided to be quiet and wait patiently until the others showed, so he sat in a bed of pine needles with his back against a large hemlock yet positioned so he could look at the river and face TJ if he decided to talk.

Soon Aqua heard the chain of a bike rattle, coming from the direction of the railroad bed behind him. He was certain without looking that it was Supper. Aqua was used to the sounds everyone's bike made. Each had its own distinct rattle, buzz, squeak, or hum, like being able to tell when his grandmother or grandfather was walking down the hallway to his bedroom, having their own rhythm or cadence. There was a couple muttered "Heys" as Supper glided over the culvert that bridged Nigger

Creek, and then rolled down from the raised railroad bed and between the cedars, where the two boys were waiting, coming to a gradual stop over the tree roots that worked as natural speed bumps. Aqua stood up from the tree. TJ stayed where he was with sort of an odd detachment. The lack of inertia by TJ in Supper's presence made Aqua curious.

"So, what's up, Sup?" Aqua spoke without taking any acknowledgment of the rhyme. It had become a cliché for the group nearly as soon as the nickname "Supper" came along.

"I've got a plan that I wanted to talk to everyone about."

"What's that?"

"Well, I wanted to wait until everybody got here," Supper replied with a restrained giddiness. Dubious, but feeling a suspense from Supper's energy, Aqua couldn't help but try to get some part of the mystery out of Supper before the others got there.

"Come on, you can tell us a little bit about it." Aqua glanced over at TJ, as if to see if he'd chime in, but TJ still made no eye contact and continued to poke the ground with a stick.

Supper paused and looked as though he was giving it serious consideration. "All right, dude," he said after a while.

"Sweet."

"But I'll have to show you something first."

"Yeah, what is it?"

Supper walked over to where the mouth of Nigger Creek formed a Y and merged with the river. He surveyed both up and down the current and pointed up stream. "You see that?"

"What?" Aqua asked, walking up behind Supper to follow the aim of his finger.

"There," he instructed urgently, as if something would be missed if Aqua didn't hurry.

Aqua came in close to Supper and squinted, even putting his hand on his shoulder to position himself for a better look. Without warning, Aqua felt a large weight plow against him, plunging him into the river. The force knocked the wind out of him, and weight consumed him, straddling itself around him. Aqua, realizing by the grasp and feel of the body around him that it was TJ, wondered immediately what game he was playing. Excuses surged through his mind and passed in an instant—this was no game.

The suspicions Aqua had shortly before, he now feared were true. Supper and TJ had planned to do something to him; maybe teach him a lesson, or worse. He had to get some air into his lungs. He had to break free from TJ's hold.

The boys tumbled in the water that seemed bottomless, though Aqua knew better. It was maybe seven feet deep in that spot, but that was deep enough to make it impossible to find any footing. The current wouldn't drag them downriver because of the way the merging of the creek stalled its flow. When TJ finally righted himself, with his arms still around Aqua, Aqua felt a chance that he'd be able to get some air on the surface, but another pair of hands were in the water, pulling down on him. It was Supper, and Aqua knew now that he was going to be the next one killed. This was the price he had to pay for killing the little boy. Now he had to answer for his sins. The things he had done were all wrong, and he should've said something, or never participated in the first place. If he were a real superhero, he would have. He would've spoke out against his friends and their atrocities. *Or was it simply his time? Was there a divine reason for this?*

Aqua wondered if this was the last the world would ever see of him, like the fudgies they drowned before him. What would his grandparents think? Would Pa be disappointed in him for not being a better swimmer? Aqua always bragged to him how good he was. Would his mother commit suicide, or did she even care that much? What were all those people thinking before they drowned? That they should just give up? Could they have made it if they pushed themselves just a little longer? Aqua's lungs needed to expand, to take in anything, even if it was water. The urge was so strong that it seemed as though his chest had more control over his mouth than the muscles in his jaws did. Aqua squirmed and wriggled to break free, but the effort didn't help. Supper must have been anchored to something to gain leverage and keep the three of them from drifting. Aqua needed to breathe, just one deep breath of air to regain his strength. He felt a stump or a root with the toe of his tennis shoe. If he could be pushed down just a little more, he might be able to launch himself against it, and then maybe get to the surface for at least a second to take in some air, dragging TJ and Supper with him. Although he could barely subdue the determination to suck in water, Aqua relaxed a moment, going limp, thinking both Supper and TJ might try to submerge him deeper when they felt his body relax—and they did. Aqua's feet came down firm and flat on the wide root or log, and even farther still in order to bend his knees. He thrust himself upward, carrying TJ with him on his back and breaking the hold Supper had on him, but TJ reached quickly with one hand and pulled Aqua's head back down, but not before he had the chance to clear the surface and take that one re-energizing breath. The desperation and struggle resumed, and Aqua felt he could no longer combat the need to suck something into his lungs and give them the gift to expand. Suddenly, harmony and a lucidity replaced all his senses. The tight squeeze TJ had around him couldn't keep his body cavity from growing. An immortal strength rushed through Aqua's mind, accelerating his neural impulses. Through his veins, new blood cells surged, an enhanced form of eosinophils, neutrophils, monocytes, lymphocytes, and basophils. The rate of his heart pumped triumphantly, and he broke free.

"Cramp!" TJ shouted, or maybe pleaded, as his head was tilted back, ears submerged, and water spraying away from his lips, as the final bit of pressure could be exhausted before the involuntary movement of the diaphragm, creating a vacuum of only water.

Supper, still flailing toward Aqua in the churning water, couldn't see the metamorphic transition that Aqua felt, and it wasn't until Aqua jettisoned out of the river—*SHOOM*—and onto the bank that Supper witnessed the impossible and the horrifying turn of events.

"Oh my God!" Supper gasped. "What happened?"

CHAPTER 5

As a diehard Piston fan, Ry thought the basement of the church would've been uncomfortable for any NBA player. The drop ceiling that had been put in to hide the joists made it seem too short, especially now that Ry had hit his growth spurt. It didn't seem that way when he was in preschool, but he couldn't remember a time he had been in the basement since then, either. He wanted to mention it to his friends, but no one looked as though they wanted to talk, or everyone looked as though they shouldn't talk, sitting as far away from each other as possible in their old classroom, now used by another generation of preschoolers who may or may not grow up together. With strict orders to stay seated and in the classroom, everyone's parents were down the hall and in the conference room, with the door shut.

Beyond the door, among the adults, the mood was even more somber and contentious as the Baltrusses entered and sat down in the two open chairs nearest the exit. Mr. Baltruss hung his liquid oxygen device over the back of the chair, but still remained tethered to it with the cannula. Mrs. Troman and Miss Moby were still trying to control their breathing from their previous sobbing. Most eyes were swollen. Despair, shock, and abandonment hung in the air as if supplied by the heating ducts. Some held on to those next to them, while a couple of the others remained separated, as if nurturing seemed vulgar. Minister Troman was one of those, sitting at the head of the table, but not unaware that everyone in the room was focusing their attention mostly at him. Mrs. Troman, sitting to his right, looked as though she was trying to lean toward him, but cautioned herself, just shy of touching his arm, as he had them on the table with his hands clasped together, suggesting a defiance. Miss Moby, to the minister's left, was leaning back in the chair with her arms crossed, occasionally dabbing her face with the tissue she had in one hand. Next to her sat the Arbuckles. With an open chair in between, at the opposite end of the table from Mr. Troman, sat Aqua's grandfather, Mr. Baltruss. To the left of him was Mrs. Baltruss, followed by the Devoses, then the Bunkers.

"I'm sorry, John," Neil Bunker said regretfully to Mr. Troman, "but that's my honest professional opinion. That long without being resuscitated, is more than likely going to result in some damage. The good thing is, the river is cold, and that could increase his odds, but still, he was without oxygen for a little over fifteen minutes. Just realize you need to be prepared." Neil's words ended like a floating feather, quietly, passively, and undetermined. Mr. Troman nodded numbly, only staring at the surface of the table. There was silence, while most glanced around the table looking for someone to speak.

"I'm sorry as well, John and Crystal. TJ is in all of our prayers. But we're all here for a reason, and I think we need to start discussing this." Everyone looked astonished by Mr. Baltruss's words, and Mrs. Baltruss poked his elbow.

"Henry," Sylvia said softly, touching his arm.

Henry looked to his wife. "I'm sorry, Sylvia, but sooner or later, we all have to talk about it," he added in a voice scarred by years of abuse.

"Henry's right," Mr. Troman announced spontaneously. "We need to talk about these boys and what we're going to do."

"I can't believe my son had any part of this," Karen Moby announced, shaking her head, her voice cracking.

"None of us can," said Henry. "But they all admitted to it. They're all guilty. *We're* all guilty."

"James wouldn't have done this if he wasn't coerced. I know that." Karen spoke bitterly now, but her voice trembled.

Heather Bunker responded, quick and defensive: "I suppose you'd want to put this all on Gary?"

"Well, it's pretty clear that he started it all by killing that kid from downstate." Karen was sitting up. Her voice no longer trembled.

Heather, now showing more of her bright-white teeth when she spoke, her brows furrowed, and her husband holding onto her arm as a restraint, said, "All the boys were there, Karen. If James was any better than my son, he would've called the police. All the other boys allowed themselves to be coerced. They're all old enough to know better."

"Gary had everyone believing it was God's will!"

Henry slapped the table. "Stop it! Stop it! Stop it! None of that matters now. All of our kids are guilty in some way or another. People are dead because of them. And right now, nobody knows, other than us and them. It doesn't matter if there was a ringleader. They *killed* people! What we have to decide is, do we let the authorities know, or keep it to ourselves and figure out how to keep it a secret for the rest of our kid's lives."

"We have to do what's right," Alex Arbuckle muttered, with his eyes locked on the table.

"And what's right, Alex?" Henry challenged and fixed his gaze on Mr. Arbuckle. There was a pause, as if everyone thought answering may be a trap. "What? No answer? Is what's right calling Chief Wagner and saying 'Hey, come and arrest our boys'? 'We just found out that they've been killing people on the river during the height of the tourist season.' "

Mrs. Baltruss started to cry. "Henry, please."

"Can I just say that I'm sorry to all of you?" Neil's tone was even more somber, though he looked nervous, and with great effort, he tried making eye contact with everyone at the table as he spoke, but when he looked toward the Baltrusses, he only made eye contact with Sylvia. "I won't deny that Gary instigated most of this, but if anyone else finds out, there won't be one of those boys"—he pointed toward the other end of the building—" not spending a great deal of time locked up. Right now, there's no one besides our kids and us who know what happened this summer."

"Did the kids say anything to Blake Norton when he came over to help?" Alex asked sheepishly.

"No." John Torman's response seemed to be a surprise to everyone. But he spoke flatly, almost detached. "I got there just when the EMTs showed up. He called the house right after he called 9-1-1." John took a deep breath and looked only at Henry. "He told me that when he ran up to the house, Arthur told him that the three of them were horsing around and TJ got a cramp, then went under. When he got to the shallows of the next bend, only then were Arthur and Gary able to pull him out of the water."

Jim Devos, Ryan's father, shifted in his chair a little and cleared his throat. "Um . . . wha—I mean . . ." He seemed apprehensive, trying to find the words to ask a question.

"What is it, hon?" Sarah Devos asked puzzled.

"We all only found out about this because Arthur told his grandfather, and supposedly Arthur had . . . well . . . reservations about what was going on in the beginning. And we know the other boys pretty much agreed to that. So, what if he decided . . . that, well . . . I dunno—"

Defensively and impatiently, Henry interrupted, "Jim, are you trying to suggest that because my grandson has a conscience, he is going to go to the authorities?" He looked at Jim and continued mockingly. "Well, that's a very good question. But here's a better one to ask: Why is it that my grandson, even after two of his so-called friends tried to kill him, ran and got help and then made up a story about how the three of them were just playing?"

"Henry, we never heard my son's side of the story and probably never will." John put his hands on the edge of the table, as if to steady or contain himself. "For all anyone knows, your grandson and Neil's boy could've made the story up about TJ. He could've been the intended victim, not Arthur."

"That's bullshit, John, and you know it."

"Stop it! Please! This is my son." Crystal Troman covered her face, sobbing.

"It doesn't matter what level of wrong the boys did at this point. In the eyes of the law, they're all complicit. I think we all know this. Maybe some will get life, maybe others thirty. In any regard, it'll be a long time before we see them again." Neil spoke in a measured tone, as if talking to incurable patients and their families. "I'm just going to put this out there, and I know I speak for Heather as well, but we don't want to see our son go to jail."

"Neither do we," Alex added, while his wife, Hailey, nodded her head in agreement.

"All I know is, James is not going to jail. Period. That's all I have to say about that," Karen said to no one in particular.

Jim Devos's eyes welled up with tears. His lips quivered as he spoke. "Sarah and I have already lost one child. We don't want to lose another. I know what he did was bad, but he's not a bad kid."

There was silence, time for reflection, then Neil asked hesitantly, "John, how do you and Crystal feel?"

John and Crystal looked at one another, then Crystal was the one to speak. "Our boy is in God's hands right now. We accept his sins. And as chances are, he has atoned for his sins. And it's more than we can bear. If there were a trial, well . . . I don't know that we'd be much longer in this world. Putting any of these boys in jail is not going to bring back the lives that were taken. Those people have been in our prayers ever since we found out. We know they are all in a better place now. The best that we can do for any of our sons right now, is to keep them close, love them dearly, and keep the Lord in their lives."

Everyone looked toward Henry and Sylvia, not at once, and most not directly. However, the atmosphere was filled with eagerness. The opinion had to be unanimous.

Henry scratched under his chin, where he had more than razor stubble. He hadn't shaved in four days. That's how long it had been since TJ's drowning, and it had taken that long for the confessions to circulate among the families; the discussions and interrogations with the parents; the soul searching. "Well, I can tell you that Arthur wouldn't go to the police, and the missus and I don't want to see our grandson go to jail, either. We know he's a good boy, and a loving boy. It doesn't take much figuring that if he ended up in prison, by the time he was out, I'll probably be dead. And I agree with you, Crystal, that the damage is done. Those people aren't coming back. Nothin' any of us can do about that. But let me ask all of you, what are your sons going to take away from all of this?" There was silence. "When you go home tonight, are you just going to tell them 'You're grounded?' You gonna spank 'em? Take away their phone privileges? How do you punish a kid for murder in your own home?"

"They didn't look at it that way!" Karen snapped.

"And they're not old enough to know better," Sarah Devos added bitterly.

Henry pointed through the door. "Those boys certainly knew how to plan the killings. They were old enough to do that."

"Henry . . ." John paused and took a deep breath. "Do you know what it's going to do to all the families here if these boys get put on trial? Do you know what it's going to do to this church? To this town? What does it even matter? Everyone else thinks they were accidents anyways."

"John, do you know what it's done to the families of the victims?"

"Yeah, Henry, we do," Crystal cried. She wept harder still and put her face in her hands.

"And so do we," Jim Devos added. "I don't understand how you can stall on this, Henry. I guess I don't see how you could bear giving up Arthur, no matter what he's done wrong!"

Henry narrowed his gaze on Jim and leaned into the table. "You know, Jim, the highlight of my day was when Arthur came home and told me about *his* day. When he'd tell me about all the things he did, people he met, and what he learned, I would go to bed knowing the world was right. In recent weeks, that has been gone. I guess I should've known that when he quit talking to me about his adventures, something was wrong. I don't know that we'll ever have that again. How do you go back to that after what these boys have been through?"

"This isn't about you, Henry. It's about the boys," Heather snapped.

"Young lady, that's exactly my point. What has happened to our kids? We've lost them already."

Karen was becoming agitated and combative the more Henry spoke. "Maybe for you, Henry, but I know right where my son is, and where he needs to be."

"Look, Henry, if we all voted on this, would you go along with the majority opinion?" Neil asked.

"Neil, you fool, we already know what the majority wants." Henry chuckled halfheartedly.

"Okay, then, Henry," Neil replied, "I'll be blunt. We'd all like to know. What are your and Sylvia's plans with Arthur? But, first, how do you feel about this, Sylvia? We haven't heard from you yet."

"How do I feel about this?" Sylvia asked vacantly. "I don't know that I have the right answer on what to do with these boys, but I do know that none of us would be here if it wasn't for your little sociopath." Everyone seemed momentarily stunned. "But now that the damage is done, and these boys were robbed of their innocence and beauty, there are no clear choices, so I'll let my husband decide. I certainly trust his opinion over anyone in this room."

"Sociopath?" Heather responded. "Your precious grandson killed a younger boy all on his own!"

"Heather's right," Hailey interjected quickly, as if sticking up for an older sister.

Henry was enraged by the accusation. "He was trying to stop the boy from yelling to protect his so-called friends. You know this!"

"Well, holding him underwater until he drowns is very effective," Heather shot back.

There were exchanges across the table simultaneously, along with name-calling such as "bitch," "son-of-a-bitch," "accomplice," "murderer," then a knock came at the door leading into the hallway. Everyone quieted down immediately. Henry was closest and stood up to answer it. All five boys were standing in the hallway, appearing wide-eyed and worried.

"What is it fellows?" Henry asked.

Aqua answered apprehensively, "We heard a lot of yelling in here, Pa, and was wondering if everything was okay."

"Yeah, everything is fine, buddy. Everyone just got a little excited. Now, why don't you all go back and sit in the classroom? We should be done here pretty soon." All the boys turned around to head back except Supper. who was in the back of the group. He took a couple of steps closer to Henry, his eyes watering.

"Mr. Baltruss," he said shakily and quietly, out of earshot from everyone else in the room.

"Yeah, Gary, what is it?" Henry asked with barely restrained contempt.

"I just wanted to say"—he bowed his head and choked up— "I . . . I'm sorry . . . for everything." Supper looked toward the floor, and Henry watched as a couple tears dripped onto the carpet. "I don't know what I was thinking."

Henry paused. "I know, Son." Henry took a step toward him and patted his shoulder mechanically. "It'll be all right. Now, why don't you join your friends? We'll be done here soon."

Supper turned and walked away. Henry shut the door and casually sat back down in his chair. He looked down toward the end of the table at Mr. Bunker. "If everyone here is ready, I think we should probably get this over with and vote on what we're going to do."

"Yeah, Henry, I think you're right," Neil replied.

The group decided unanimously to keep the murders to themselves, then called the boys into the room. They swore before God to maintain their silence and prayed forgiveness for the boys' transgressions. There were no goodbyes or "see ya laters" when Henry corralled Sylvia and Arthur to go home. They were the first ones who left, heading down the hall, up the steps, out the rear door, and into the twilight of the Transfiguration Church parking lot. The Baltrusses were not suspicious. They never had anything in common with other families or members, only by the friendship Arthur shared with the other boys; that, and Sylvia needed her weekly dose of the Lord on Sundays and the occasional baked goods contributions for some community charity.

The other parents stayed until they saw the headlights of Henry's Trailblazer flash through the basement window as it turned out of the drive and onto Highway 12C. At that point, Neil asked Gary to grab the other three boys and go back into the classroom. "Your mother and I have something to discuss with the other parents."

"But what about Mr. and Mrs. Baltruss, shouldn't they be here?" Supper asked curiously.

"Son, this doesn't concern them. It's something completely different."

Supper did as he was told, noting the firmness in his father's voice. Then, as the boys left, the adults sat back down at the table. John Troman took a deep breath. "So, is everyone as worried as I am?"

"We certainly are, John," Hailey Arbuckle said, replying for her husband as well, but glancing across the table at Heather. Then there seemed to be a succession of "yeahs," and "mmhmms."

John looked around the table. "Okay, then, I think we know what has to be done. We discussed this yesterday. Karen," John said directly, "you said your brother can do this for twenty thousand?"

"Actually, it may be slightly higher. That was an estimate," Karen replied, slightly embarrassed.

John was marginally surprised and suspicious. "And you didn't tell him the details of the job?"

"All I told him was I might have a job for him. And I explained vaguely what it would involve. But I didn't tell him anything more than that. He then said it would be about twenty thousand, maybe a little higher." Karen felt that everyone was studying her, and someone would call her out on her lie, but no one did.

"When would he be able to do it," Neil interjected?

"Well, he's in Detroit. He can be here in a day. He' currently out of work."

"Good," Neil replied. "I think you should call him tonight, so we can get this thing taken care of right away, before they have a chance to tell anyone. What does everyone else think?"

"I think it's a little high and I think we need a fixed price, but Sarah and I can put in sixty-five hundred," Jim Devos said.

Karen offered a thousand, which was suspect, and everyone thought she was getting a cut from the money anyway, but when John offered three thousand, Neil offered to front the rest as long as it didn't go above twenty-two thousand. Karen reassured him that if it did, she would rescind the offer. But also added that her brother was in need of some cash and probably wouldn't turn it down. The matter was settled.

For reassurance, John spoke for all when he asked Karen, "Now, your brother can definitely make this look like an accident, right?"

"Oh, definitely. He's done"—she paused— "several of these before."

"Well, then, that's that. Before we leave, I think we should have another prayer." Everyone grabbed hands around the table and bowed their heads. "Dear Lord," John began, "please take Henry, Sylvia, and young Arthur Baltruss into your wonderful kingdom when their time comes. They are kind souls. And, Lord, please guide Karen's brother . . ." John glanced over to Karen, and she sensed it.

"Eric," she added in.

". . . Eric's hands into making this as painless as possible for this family. Amen."

"Amen," all in the room echoed.

CHAPTER 6

"Hello?"

"Hi, Eric, it's Karen."

"Yeah, Sis, what's up?" Eric's tone was mechanical, bored, and without an iota of curiosity. His silence between words was intimidating to Karen. She knew her brother well and found herself speaking softer, almost at a whisper.

"Remember that thing I talked to you about the other day?" Karen tried to make her sentences short, because she knew her voice would crack if she didn't.

"Yes. And . . .?"

"The group would like to go through with it."

"The amount?"

"Fifteen thousand."

"Twenty."

"Yeah, but that means I'll have to come up with another five grand, Eric. James and I are just barely getting by now."

"Well, what about your *group*? Can't you milk some more from them?"

"No, I don't think they'll budge any more than they already have."

"Not my problem, Karen. You already know I'm doing this for far less than I normally would. And if this wasn't a big deal, you would've already said that fifteen is the max. Plus, I'm pretty sure my sis is skimming a little extra for herself."

"Okay, twenty thousand, but that means I have to come up with another five." Karen was quiet for a moment, almost expecting some sympathy from her brother, but she knew better. She also knew that if she pushed the issue, she may expose herself and give up too much.

"I'll also need gas money, plus money for a room and food."

"Sure." Karen rolled her eyes. Karen was about to give Eric the last name of the family and tell him where they lived. But Eric interrupted.

"Yeah. I'll need the money when I get there, and then you can also give me the name of the family."

Karen didn't want to see her brother, but knew it was inevitable. She certainly didn't want her son around his uncle. So, this moment was a good opportunity to set up a meeting place other than her home. "How about we meet at the ballpark?"

"Wow, Sis. You sure know how to put out the welcome mat."

"Well, I just thought that . . . you know, I mean . . . we wanna make sure no one sees us. This is a small town, and my neighbors are—"

"Relax." Eric let out a glib chuckle. He enjoyed listening to his little sister squirm. "The Park it is. I'm assuming it's easy to find."

"It is."

"I'll drive up in a day or two and call you when I get close. I've got a few things to take care of first. Just make sure you have everything I need."

"I will."

"Oh, and I'd like to hear something about the group you mentioned, Sis. This all sounds pretty intriguing."

"I'm afraid I can't, Eric. They prefer to remain anonymous."

"Okay, I get it. Maybe someday, Little Sis," Eric added facetiously, making the conversation all the more uncomfortable.

Karen couldn't wait for this to be over, for her brother to be gone. She knew him too well. When they were young, he had killed their father. It wasn't that he didn't have it coming, since Karen's father physically abused the whole family. Karen never suffered the full-on swings, but she did get the backhands, the shoves, the threats, and the degradation. Eric and their mother received the worst of it, and then, as Eric grew into his teens, he became more and more of a target for his father, with their father somehow seeing him as a male threat. However, the way Karen remembered it, Eric always made it worse, seemingly egging their father on, even at the cost of his anger being directed toward Karen and her mother. She often caught him smirking after a beating, as if he took some twisted pleasure in what had happened.

Karen and her mother were there the day Eric killed their father. Karen lied in court to protect her brother, but mostly because of their mother. The jury sympathized, giving Eric only five years, two as a juvenile and three as an adult. But Karen knew there was never any regret or remorse from her brother. It was premeditated, not reactionary. It was also barbaric, seeing and hearing her father's skull crack, and then becoming spongier and spongier with each successive hit. It was a setup by her brother, enticing their father and waiting for the first few drinks to take effect. She added the pieces together later; him setting the baseball bat by the hutch before their father got home; deliberately putting the baseball through the neighbor's window before that, so their father would be angered about having to confront the neighbor. She knew Eric orchestrated it all, so he'd have his reason, and she was sure the five years was worth it to him. One juror told the *Detroit Free Press*: "I can only imagine what that poor beautiful young man and his sister had to live through." All the neighbors corroborated the abuse.

Eric couldn't understand why his sister moved to a small town, other than, he hoped, *to get away from that nigger she shacked up with*. The people north were ridiculous, ignorant hicks. They were weak, hiding from people behind their picket fences, timid smiles, and desperate "good mornings," as if the greeting would bless them and protect them through the day. The farther north, away from the cities, Eric drove, the more contemptuous he became, driving his Jeep through the middle of the night. Stopping for gas off the highway, he found a young man tending the EZ-Mart alone. He was a very young-looking twenty-something, slim, with hair hanging over one side of his face. He had that uninterested look about him, as if he were spoiled by privilege, but Eric knew better. He wouldn't be working here, pulling the midnight shift, if he was. The boy-man had to have been at least twenty-one but looked as though he was sixteen. He was vulnerable, but there were cameras everywhere. *What are the chances they're on? Are they just there for show?* Eric thought. The temptation to attack him was overwhelming. Eric paused at the counter, momentarily causing the young man concern.

"Sir? Sir?"

Eric looked into the boy's eyes and glared for a moment longer. He knew he couldn't defend himself. He would collapse under Eric's strength. It wouldn't matter if he had martial arts training, he was just too small, too slight. Eric shook his head and took a deep breath. "Sorry, it's been a long drive. I guess I need to get some sleep."

"Our coffee is only a buck twenty-five for a large," the boy replied, pushing the bangs away from his eyes, only to have them drop immediately back in front of his face.

Eric couldn't help but think how tender and inviting the boy looked, as if the brushing aside of his hair and the momentary eye contact were seductive gestures, maybe flirting or teasing.

"Ah, no, thanks." He glanced at the name tag on the front of the boy's shirt. "Jeremy, I don't care for coffee. I guess I'll just look for a place to stop for the night."

Farther down the highway, Eric couldn't wait any longer. He pulled over to the side of the rode and masturbated to the thought of what he could have so easily done to that boy. There were no other cars this time of night in the middle of the week. Anyone who did drive by wouldn't be able to see anything anyway. It was too dark; plus, he had a map on the passenger seat he could lay across his lap if someone stopped to see if he needed help.

You stupid fucking little bitch. You fucking whore. Eric imagined himself hitting the attendant again and again, then pulling his hair while he sodomized Jeremy, all while the boy was begging Eric to stop and promising to do anything for him. He imagined raping him in front of faceless onlookers, all of whom were too shocked and too weak to do anything. All in fear of Eric's power and control. Then in a pulsating spurt, he came on the blue paper towels he had pulled from the window wash at the gas station.

"You goddamn stupid bitch. You're fucking worthless," Eric said disgustedly, as he squeezed the last of his semen onto the paper.

Once he was back on the road, Eric drove for another hour and a half. In thirty-five minutes, according to his TomTom, he would be at his destination. He heard the thunder, then saw the lightning strike, miles ahead of him. The sky directly above him was still clear—he could see the stars. Then, suddenly, glancing down at the road once again, he saw that there was a cow elk in his lane, and a calf off on the shoulder. He braked and swerved, but not soon enough. For that flash of an instant, in its confusion, the cow jumped into the path of the car, flipping, with its upper back, neck, and head crashing through the windshield. Eric raised his right arm to try to protect his face, but the action fractured his humerus, jaw, and dislocated his shoulder. The car careened off the road and down a twenty-foot sloping ravine, the airbag burst, pressing chunks of glass into his scalp, forehead, and cheeks, then the Jeep toppled over on its roof into a creek bed that crossed perpendicular under the highway.

Eric was upside down, held in by his seat belt. The creek was shallow, but because the roof was partially crushed and the car had landed centered in the creek, water quickly filled it. It soon covered his forehead. Momentarily unconscious because of the blow to his jaw, Eric was soon revived by the water. He could tilt his head out of the water. He began to survey his situation, then the pain struck him. He couldn't move his right arm or clench his jaw. Blood was streaming down his face from the bits of glass embedded in his cheeks. The blood was getting into his eyes, stinging, making it difficult to see. He wiped his eyes free with his left hand and tried looking around again, but more blood blocked his line of sight. He yelled and yelled, and tried to form the word "help," but he could barely move his jaw, and forming the word proved impossible, no matter how hard or how many times he tried. Hearing a car whiz by in the distance and noting how quickly the sound disappeared, Eric knew there was no chance anyone would hear him. *Maybe they can see my lights.* He reached with his left hand through the steering wheel. The keys were still on. He fumbled with the light switch. Nothing. He yelled again. What Eric didn't know was that even if his lights worked, no one could see him from the road—he had no way of knowing just how far he had dropped. If no one could hear or see him from the road, then maybe there was a house nearby, he found himself hoping. But there wasn't. The closest building was a mile away. Surrounding him was a cedar swamp, marsh, and ponds, a popular duck sanctuary.

The pain was becoming intolerable. He knew he couldn't hang upside down much longer. Somehow, he had to get his seat belt unfastened, but how? He could use his left arm to help alleviate some of his body weight by pushing on the roof of the car, but he had no control or strength in his right arm. Eric was a strong man. However, at six two and two hundred sixty-two pounds, without the use of one arm to take some pressure off, it made unsnapping the buckle impossible. Between the jolts of pain, he was beginning to feel groggy. Either the car was sinking, or the creek was rising. Because of the sound of the creek near his ears, he hadn't noticed that it was raining, but the rain was getting heavier and heavier.

The creek was rising an inch or two by the hour, but in Eric's confined position, it seemed like much more. It was still dark, and Eric was getting a cramp in his neck. It was getting more and more difficult to bend. "Helllll! Helllllp . . .!" Eric cried to no one, as the noise barely traveled beyond the crest of the ditch. The rain stopped, and the sky cleared. It was nearly six o'clock. Although it was still shaded in the ravine, he could see the daylight coming.

Through the passenger side window, he could make out the dead elk, lying on the bank, face toward him and staring. He saw some movement nearby, but just before he yelled, praying that whoever it was could help him, he realized it was the calf he had seen on the shoulder of the road before he went down the ravine. It was nudging its mother, trying to get her to move, still lingering to see if its only companion and protector was going to revive and they could go on for their daily forage through the swamp and marsh, eventually bedding down in some tall grass to take a rest in the sunlight.

Using his left hand, Eric was able to pull his leg up tight enough to his chest to get his foot against the dashboard. Pressing himself hard into his seat, he reached across his chest for the buckle. The seat belt slackened. He was able to scratch at the top of the buckle, but just couldn't reach the button. The strain and his condition exhausted him. He stopped to get his breath, but the water made it hard to breathe and simultaneously bend his neck at a sharp enough angle to remain above the waterline, especially since his neck was becoming stiff from the jolt his head had taken in the crash. He tried again, yelling through the pain, with all the strength he could muster. He had to push his head back underwater, then let some air out of his lungs so his chest would deflate, giving his left arm slightly more freedom. He finally pressed the button, and the seat belt released. Eric slid down onto the roof and into the water. His left arm had to do most of the work, because his legs still had very little freedom. He then clawed himself toward the passenger side window, which was the only opening he could see to get through.

Once he was free from the car and lying on the bank next to the elk, Eric yelled. He rested but passed out. It was only going to be for a moment, because he knew he had to get up on the road and get help. He woke shivering uncontrollably. It was early August, but the mornings were unnaturally cooler than normal, and adding in being drenched from the creek, hypothermia was setting in. Eric made his way up the steep ditch onto the shoulder of the highway, where the sun was now shining. He sat on the guardrail shaking uncontrollably but relishing the sun and sitting with his face toward it, sensing he could absorb more of its heat this way.

Eric heard a car and signaled with his left arm. It kept going. Then he signaled another and another. He got up and stood closer to the shoulder. He had no way of knowing that where he was standing—on a curve in a northbound lane, where the road was turning out of the east and back toward the north, and just coming up out of a valley—made it almost impossible to see him. Unless the driver was wearing sunglasses to avoid the glare, it would be too late to see Eric until he was abreast of the car or in the rearview mirror. Eric couldn't understand why no one was slowing down and stopping. He needed help. Someone had to get him medical attention.

Dane went downstate early, before the semester started. It was his second year of college, and this year, he was moving into a five-bedroom apartment house. His parents helped him move in a week earlier. He had a mini fridge from the year before that he had used in his dorm room. After realizing the house refrigerator wasn't big enough or practical enough for five young guys, he decided to get the mini fridge. Dane was traveling early so he could pick up the fridge, then be back down in time to have Xbox night with his new roommates. Eric was over the white line, off the shoulder. Dane saw him too late, but at least soon enough not to hit him head-on. Instead, Eric was hit with the rear panel and rear passenger side window of the Subaru. The impact sent him spinning through the air like a figure skater losing control and body coordination right after executing a triple axel, propelling him back over the guardrail, where he landed on the bottom of his overturned car.

CHAPTER 7

The last thing Eric remembered was the sunlight, and that was what he thought he was seeing when he first opened his eyes in the brightness of the hospital and tried to focus. He had a fractured pelvis, punctured spleen, collapsed lung, three fractured ribs, shattered left wrist and forearm, fractured femur, a concussion, and a multitude of lacerations. He was in traction, wrapped, strapped, tube fed, inserted with a catheter, and attached to monitors. While he was unconscious, they had re-inflated his lung, and his jaw had been reset and wired shut. Eric's initial appearance was reminiscent of an old comedy movie, in which the bumbling protagonist or foiled villain either saved the day or was denied of his sinister vision, but at the cost of being put in a full body cast.

Besides part time at the grocery store, Karen also worked at a small paper plant that recycled pulp into tissue paper, in the small industrial park on the outskirt of town. Her shift had just started, and she was just getting the small fork truck to pick up a two-thousand-pound roll of tissue paper from the staging area and put it on the wrapped wheel, when her supervisor called her into the break area for a phone call. At first, she thought it was her brother, whom she was expecting, because he was supposed to be in town already. The person on the other end of the call, though, was a stranger to her. He identified himself as a member of the sheriff's department. The first thing he asked her was if she knew someone named Eric Zender. She paused. Zender was her maiden name. She had kept the name Moby after she married, then divorced, James's father. She didn't want anyone to remember her or make the connection to her past. That's one of the reasons she had married a black man. Karen was aware it would upset her brother, and more still, make her father roll over in his grave.

"Yes," Karen answered reluctantly, thinking that she may be implicating herself to something. But to lie about their relationship would ultimately be exposed anyway.

"And what is your relationship to Eric?"

"Well, he's my brother. Why?"

"It appears your brother was involved in an auto accident . . ."

What was said immediately after that Karen didn't hear. She didn't even care if the voice said he was dead. She was just relieved to know that she wasn't being called in for questioning. That the authorities hadn't somehow found out about their plot to murder the Baltrusses. And there was some relief that the plot was stalled. Not that she didn't still want it to be done to protect her boy's future, but she knew that, in some way, if her brother did this thing, it would be another secret to add to that dark, disturbing past with him, and keep their estranged bond as siblings.

"I'm sorry, what's that?"

"We found your name and number in his wallet. It was the only one in there. Is there anyone else you may know of that we should call? Maybe a spouse, children, parent?"

As much as she wanted as little to do with Eric as possible, to have their mother involved right now would be cruel and confusing. Although Karen had no desire to speak to her mother again, she also felt that her mother had paid a big enough price, and since it wasn't essential, she be involved, that's the least Karen could do. And oddly, this may be a debt she could pay and be done with her mother forever. One last chain that anchored her to that past would be released and allow her to deal with her new set of troubles.

"Actually, I'm probably the only contact that I know of right now. Why, what happened?"

"Well, as I stated, your brother is in stable condition, however, it would be a good idea for someone who knows him to come up to the hospital as soon as possible. Would you be willing to do that for us?"

What choice did Karen really have? She had called him. And what would he say to anyone if she didn't show? What condition was he in, and would he come after her and James if she ignored him? He may even be delirious and say something incriminating without even meaning to.

"Yeah, I can be at the hospital in about an hour."

"Thank you."

When Karen got to the hospital room, Eric was asleep, sedated. She had her son with her. She didn't want him to be there, but because of recent events, she didn't want him alone, either.

"Wow, Uncle Eric looks really messed up," Moe mumbled to his mother.

"Yeah."

"All of that from just hitting a deer?"

"It wasn't a deer. It was an elk," Karen corrected Moe.

"Yeah, but they ain't that much bigger."

"Well, we don't know the circumstances."

"He doesn't look like he can feed himself, or walk, or do much of anything," Moe said in astonishment.

"Yeah, I know," Karen replied dejectedly, thinking of the implications of Eric's condition.

Moe sat down in an open chair against the wall, under the on-call board, where the attending nurses and techs put their names. It was a double-bed room, but Eric was currently the only patient, and occupying the bed by the window. "Mom, did you know Uncle Eric was up here? Was he coming to visit or something?"

"I don't know why he's here," Karen answered sharply.

It was no secret to Moe that his mother had little love for her brother. However, he never really knew the reason. He had his suspicions, thinking it had something to do with his grandfather. Any time he tried coming near the topic with his mother, she became very defensive, so it was just never talked about. Moe resigned himself to his handheld Playstation, and periodically studied his mother while they sat in the hospital room, waiting for his uncle to come around. The nurses and techs darted in and out, which, on occasion, caused Uncle Eric to stir. The attending physician walked in once and spoke to Karen in hushed tones that Moe could not completely understand.

Finally, at a point when there were no hospital staff around, Eric's eyelids fluttered, and his vision came into focus. First, he stared up at the ceiling tiles, then at the track that held the curtain separating the beds. On the spacious windowsill sat a brown, lanky boy in jeans and a gray T-shirt, with curly, bushy hair, punching buttons on what looked like a large cell phone in the palms of his hands. The face looked familiar, but Eric couldn't make out why. The last time Eric saw his sister's kid was when he was six, and at that time, he had been a boxy-looking little boy.

Karen was filing her nails, needing the motion and rhythm of something to help organize her thoughts, when she happened to look up and see her brother staring at her. She froze. She hoped that it was a fluke, that he may have been in a dream state, or that he had lapsed into some sort of coma and his eye movements were just a phantom response, but his cold, sharp blue eyes were too penetrating, too focused. Karen realized she was holding her breath, as if holding still to evade the attack of a mountain lion that she had discovered was circling her camp. Eric was awake. His head shifted to better see Moe, then he made the connection.

"Hey, Eric," Karen said in a falsely cheerful tone, cautiously upbeat.

Moe looked up from his game, waiting for his uncle to acknowledge him. When Eric turned his head slightly to give Moe a glance, he returned an uncomfortable wave and nod. Karen stepped toward Eric's bed.

"How are you doing?" Eric only stared at Karen. She knew it was a stupid question. "Can you talk?"

Eric's jaw was braced shut, but he spoke through clenched teeth. "Sure . . . What do you want to talk about?"

Even through his wrapped jaw, bandaged face, and limitations, Karen and Moe both could sense the sarcasm and bitterness.

"Well, the doctor said with time and some therapy, you should eventually make a full recovery."

"Yeah? What the hell does 'eventually' mean?" With his teeth clenched, the reply made Eric sound even angrier. "Thanks a lot, Sis. It's because of you that I'm in this situation. Where's the fucking doctor? Get the fucking doctor in here!"

Karen was alarmed and didn't want Eric to say any more. She thought to get Moe out of the room first, so she could talk to Eric quietly and no one else could hear. "James, why don't you go out into the waiting room?"

Moe was puzzled by what Eric had said. "What does he mean that this is your fault . . .?"

"Nothing! It's probably just the medication," Karen snapped. "Just do what I say."

"But . . ."

"Now!" Karen interrupted, giving her son a hard look.

"Okay, okay, I'm going. Geez." Moe marched out of the room.

Karen turned to Eric and moved in closer to him. There was nothing he could do to her physically, being wrapped, strapped, and immobilized the way he was now was the time to try to reason with him. "Eric, please, you have to be careful what you say in front of anyone. James is a smart kid and picks up on everything."

"Even being a dime-store nigger, as good ole Dad would say?" Eric gave Karen a hard stare, knowing she couldn't act out her response, and knowing he had her in a precarious situation.

"Please, please, don't do this, Eric. I promise I'll do everything I can to try to help you out," Karen pleaded quietly. She knew she couldn't give Eric any more information. She certainly couldn't tell him why she had hired him to kill the Baltrusses now. Any slip to anyone could bring on suspicion and questions, and ultimately expose her son's involvement in the killings. If Eric had any more information, he would use it as leverage and blackmail. She had to be careful not to upset him. Karen needed to buy time and think this whole mess through.

"Don't get your panties in a twist there, Sis. But, yeah, you're gonna help me get out of this shit. That goes without saying," he spat out through his clenched teeth as saliva built up in his mouth.

There was a startling rap on the open door, and a young-looking Middle Eastern female doctor entered the room. She smiled and walked into the room mechanically, routinely, as if this were her fiftieth stop for the afternoon, and given the wrong paperwork, she could've easily mistaken Eric for a child with an appendix issue. She asked the typical questions, showed the generic pleasantries, and after familiarizing herself with Eric's chart, offered the basic, "Well, everything seems to be looking good," and "Right now, we'd like to see you get plenty of rest." The doctor appeared to be artful in deflecting Eric's impatience. "We're doing everything we can. You've been through quite an ordeal, and considering the circumstances, have been very lucky."

That evening, leaving Moe home alone, saying she was running up to the store, Karen was able to break away and meet with Minister Troman and Neil Bunker in the basement of the church. They went to the same room and sat at the same table where they had last met with Henry and Sylvia Baltruss. The three leaned in toward each other, on their elbows at the end of the table, farthest away from the door.

"So, you swear before God that you never mentioned yet to your brother any names or details on who or why you asked him to come up and do this job?" John Troman asked desperately, like a child. Neil almost expected him to follow it with, "Cross your heart?"

"No, honest, I swear," Karen lied smoothly.

"Well, you certainly can't say anything now," Neil interjected.

John shook his head. "This is terrible."

"You think I don't know this, John? Now I have to take care of my brother until he's well enough to leave, which could be months. Plus, I know he's going to want to be compensated whether he does the job or not."

"Wait a minute now." Neil leaned back in his chair. "It's nobody's fault but his own that he got into an accident. He doesn't deserve anything for this!"

"You don't know my brother. He's a sociopath. If he doesn't get his way, he'll cause trouble for us."

"Well, I'm sorry, Karen, but I don't know how he can cause trouble for *us* if you don't tell him anything. And I'm pretty sure you won't if it means implicating James." Neil finished with an unflinching stare at Karen. "Am I right?"

As she glanced over at John and saw he had the same uncompromising stare, Karen suddenly felt abandoned on an unfriendly island. "Yeah, but . . . I don't have any money to give to Eric."

"Look, hon," John spoke reassuringly, "right now, your brother doesn't know anything. So, no matter what he says, there is nothing he can hold against you. Correct? Besides, no crime has been committed. I can give you about five hundred to help a little, but that's about it. And that means adjusting the church funds a little, if you know what I mean."

John and Karen looked to Neil. He looked as though he felt no pressure, still eyeing Karen steadily. "I can give you five hundred as well, but that's it from me too. I'm sorry."

Karen knew she had no leverage to argue. She felt abandoned and insignificant. The minister and Neil were right. Her mind raced out of the room, already working on the strategy for dealing with her brother, preparing herself mentally. She thought of the possibility of paying him in installments after he was better. If she coddled him and really nurtured him, maybe she could get away with giving him only a small stipend. Or maybe, just maybe, she could kill the Baltrusses herself and collect the money. And maybe she could still use her brother to help set it up and plan the murders. Then again, he had no horse in this race, and if he knew any details, could easily use it as blackmail. But still, if nothing was done, would Henry and Sylvia talk to the authorities and put her beautiful James in jeopardy? Something *had* to be done. She needed to be certain that her son would never be taken away.

"Well, what about the Baltrusses? I mean, we still have to come up with a plan to make sure they don't talk, right?"

"Karen," John began, resigned and reflective, "the good Lord gave us a sign, which is that it's in his hands now. I believe that it was by God's will that your brother was forced off the road. Clearly, we need to step aside and let him handle things now."

"Wait. You mean we're going to take the risk that Henry just might decide to throw all of the boys under the bus and destroy all of our lives, because he thinks it's the right thing to do?"

"I just think it's divine intervention that your brother crashed his car, and we should take it as a sign. There is a reason for everything. God has a plan."

Karen envisioned her loving son being taken away in handcuffs, and the news highlights about young serial killers. "And God gave us free will, John! I don't think he has a plan for everything. If he did, I think he would be a little more competent than to allow some stupid young boys to drown tourists."

"Wait a minute, Karen!" John demanded. "You are being blasphemous."

"I think John is absolutely right," Neil snapped quickly. "This is something we are just going to have to let go. I don't think it's anything we need to discuss further."

"Wait a minute. I know what's going on here. If Henry says anything, the rest of you are going to blame the black kid and the boy whose parents abandoned him." Karen noticed Neil's gaze drop. "You've already talked this over with the other parents and are probably coaching your kids for an alibi, aren't you!"

"Karen, come on, you're being irrational and paranoid," John said, like a parent trying to calm the fears of a child claiming there was a monster under the bed.

Like so many of all other situations in her life, Karen knew that she was at a cul-de-sac in her defense. No matter how logical, informative, or desperate she came across, she was going to be shut down or not taken seriously. There was a long pause while the trio anticipated a response from each other. John seemed about to add something, taking a deep breath, but ended up doing nothing more than releasing a barely vocal "ah" from the back of his throat.

With eyes downward in a defeated gaze, Karen sighed. "Well, I guess I better get home. I have to get James some dinner." Karen didn't look at Neil Bunker or Minister Troman. She didn't want to, and it wouldn't matter if she did. They were firm in their decision. It was more than obvious. Anything said beyond this point would be begging, and she knew that. She also knew that it would only fortify their position. Karen slung her purse over her shoulder, pushed her chair back under the table, and walked out of the room. Whatever discussion the two men were going to have with each other after she left would be irrelevant. Karen had to deal with her situation day by day now, considering only the moment. It crossed her mind to talk with Henry and Sylvia, creating an alliance of sorts, but she knew that would be particularly insulting to Henry, and could possibly force his hand even more if he knew of any plot. Karen would simply have to deal with the daily uncertainty for the months to come and get used to having her sociopathic brother around the house. It would be survival for her and James. She had to shut down her senses and save her energy, as she had done so often before, living her life on autopilot until things were safe again. *Why, why,* she thought, *was God punishing her?*

What Karen didn't know was that Henry no longer had any desire or second thoughts of going to the authorities. Sylvia pleaded with him the same night they had the meeting in the church, not to have their grandson taken away. She pleaded so passionately that it made her sick. By coincidence, or perhaps the tragic reality she was now forced to endure, it was a sickness she would never recover from. Ten days after the meeting, and while Eric was still in the hospital, Sylvia suffered a debilitating stroke. From there on, it seemed to Henry, Sylvia made no effort to recover, as if to sacrifice herself for her grandchild's sins.

Five days after Sylvia had the stroke, Eric was discharged from the hospital and released into Karen's care. Medicaid allowed a maximum of one month for rental on a hospital bed for the home. Karen had the Service Technician who delivered the bed set it up in the living room. Mostly because that was the only place in her double-wide trailer where there was enough room; plus, it was the most convenient location in the home. When Karen was in Eric's room just before the discharge, the physician appeared optimistic in the recovery process for Eric and felt that he should be ambulatory within a month, and at the latest, six weeks. Karen was slightly relieved and felt that was a time frame she may be able to endure. Her worry was James and what Eric may say to him to try to manipulate him. She wished that she could have James stay with someone else for that period, but she had no real family to speak of now. She'd had a boyfriend for a while, but he'd only work long enough at a job to be able to collect unemployment, forcing the employer to fire him by incompetence or laziness as soon as he knew he could collect on the benefits. Then, he'd spend the money he'd saved on hunting and fishing. He never invited James along or contributed to rent and groceries. While Karen was crying for him to leave, in an attempt to defend himself, he declared, "I help this family out all the time! Because of me you have a freezer full of venison, don't ya! . . . Ungrateful bitch." Both Karen and James hated venison and would forcibly choke it down only out of politeness.

In the past she could've asked the Baltrusses, knowing what good friends James and Arthur had been, but now, well, there was no reason to even entertain the idea. Karen would simply have to be on her guard every minute, which would be very precarious. On one hand, she didn't want him hanging out with a lot of kids at school activities and possibly confiding in someone about what he and the other boys had done. Now that the new school year was set to begin in less than a week, he would have plenty of opportunity to do that anyway. On the other hand, she didn't want him spending much time alone with Uncle Eric, as she knew how charismatic her brother could be, and how he could give people a false sense of security, possibly causing James to bait Eric into more questioning.

"Wow, Sis, this isn't too bad for a single mom," Eric said through his wired teeth as two EMTs brought him in on a stretcher.

"Thanks," Karen replied automatically, while focusing on escorting the ambulance team down the hallway and into the living room, where Eric's hospital bed awaited him next to the bay window that looked out over the quarter-acre front yard. James stood off to the side with his hands in his pockets, waiting to be of assistance. The hospital bed was raised to a comfortable level to transfer Eric with little to no lifting, instead requiring only some sliding and skooching.

After Eric was settled in the bed, the EMTs left, Karen thanking them and escorting them to the door before returning to the living room. Just as Karen was asking Eric if he needed anything, James handed him the remote for the television.

"Here ya go, Uncle Eric."

"Well, thanks, amigo. Look at me, getting five-star service." Karen couldn't tell if he was trying to be pleasant or mocking. "Ah, yeah, I will have a glass of juice if you have some, Sis."

"I have orange, grape, or V8, which do you want?" Karen asked, walking around the partition into the kitchen.

"Grape?" Eric blurted in a disgusted tone loud enough for Karen to hear him on the other side of the wall. "Who the hell drinks grape?"

Defiantly, James responded, "I do."

Eric looked over his shoulder where James was standing and leaning his hip against the arm of the loveseat. He could see that James was offended.

"Orange juice sounds good to me," Eric shouted as best he could. Then he looked back over at James, and in a quieter voice, so Karen couldn't hear, he said, "Don't worry, little man, I didn't mean anything by it."

James turned around and disappeared into the opposite hallway leading into his bedroom. Karen came around the partition and into the living room with a glass of orange juice and a straw. "Here ya go," she said, handing the drink to Eric.

CHAPTER 8

It was a Saturday. In a little over a week, Moe would be back in school. He hadn't seen any of his friends since the night that the parents had their meeting in the basement of the church. His mother no longer took him to Sunday sermons. He was able to e-mail Aqua to say he was sorry to hear about his grandmother, but never got a response. Moe's mother had put such restrictions on computer time that even sending the e-mail had been hard to do without being caught. She had forced him to delete his MySpace account, and always made sure take the power cord to the computer with her when she left the house. Even though the boy was filled with a great deal of uncertainty, he still desperately wanted to get back to school. He *needed* to get back to school. His mother worked the early shift at the factory part time and was home by a little after noon, ate lunch, and when she went to her second job at the grocery store, and Moe was forced to go with her.

He usually stayed up late and slept in late, so Moe's contact alone with his Uncle Eric was minimal. His mother told him to keep away from his uncle as much as possible, because during his recovery, his behavior might seem a little odd. Moe did find his behavior "a little odd," but he wasn't sure why. Eric seemed nice enough, complimenting often, asking questions about his music and seeming interested in what his tastes were. One morning, around eleven, Moe dashed through the living room without his shirt on to get a bowl of cereal, passing in front of the television while Eric was channel surfing. Karen had left early to go grocery shopping, expecting to beat the weekend rush on a sale they were having at a Meijer's forty miles from town. Unfortunately, everyone else got the same flyer in a ninety-mile radius and had the same idea.

"Wow," Eric said. "You never told me you worked out."

Moe paused. "Wha-whaddya mean?"

"You have a pretty good form for a young man your age. Sturdy arms, broad chest. Do you lift weights?"

All of a sudden feeling self-conscious, but flattered, Moe felt compelled to respond. "Not really, but I do pushups and that kind of stuff."

"Show me them biceps." Moe flexed his right arm. "Holy cow," Eric exclaimed. "Come here and let me see." Moe took the four steps toward Eric's bed with his muscle still flexed. Eric reached up and squeezed it between his thumb and middle finger. "Man, *that* is tight."

"Thanks." Moe relaxed his arm.

"No kidding, as soon as I get all these braces off, you're going to have to show me your workout routine, because I'd like to get in shape like you, man. Wanna look good for the ladies, if you know what I mean?"

"Sure," Moe replied, flashing a modest smile, standing a little straighter, and then stepping away awkwardly before vanishing behind the partition into the kitchen.

"I mean it, dude. You're gonna have to show me how you do it," Eric said with false enthusiasm, deceptively slipping his hand under the sheet to squeeze his crotch.

"Yeah, sure," Moe shouted back from the kitchen.

Eric was starting to get around a little more each day, using his walker with the forearm attachment. It *was* slow for him to complete the most minor tasks, but he had all day to do them. Karen was surprised that he wasn't more demanding and couldn't help wondering why. She knew her brother better than anyone, and knew he was always thinking, always calculating, and always figured that the world owed him. If anyone felt short-changed, it was him. What puzzled Karen most was that her brother had yet to ask what the "job" was and who the people were who needed to be "taken care of." She studied James closely every day for signs that Eric may have pried him for details. However, she was careful not to question him, knowing that would cause suspicion and confusion for him too. Then, when she wasn't worrying about her brother, she still agonized over what James must be going through. And what was she going to do once he went back to school? She would have no way of intercepting any relationships he may want to resume or begin. Would he start hanging out with his old friends again? And if he did, would that be so bad? He was going into the ninth grade. It would be four years before he was out of high school. Karen prayed and sobbed at the end of her bed every night, just like she had as a girl, before Eric killed her father. But would there be a price to pay for her prayers? A condition? A clause, like having her brother leering over her shoulder for the rest of her life? Karen knew she couldn't sit on the edge of her seat anymore with James. He would come to resent her, and he was the only good thing in her life. He was her only hope. She wanted to give him a little more freedom, so when he asked her if he could go for a bike ride, she agreed. But she asked him to call occasionally to check in, giving him her cell phone, since she had the land line and would be in the house all day cleaning and preparing a roast in the Crock-Pot that they could eat for the weekend. She could blend the potatoes, carrots, broth, and meat in small portions for Eric. It was sort of a special occasion, as she had received a fifteen-cent hourly raise at the screen shop.

The day was bright, with little wisps of clouds in the sky like skips on a freshly painted wall, evidence that the painter only put on one coat. These were the best days of summer, when the heat was dry. The shade from the trees made a difference, whereas, when it was humid, it only kept the eyes from squinting. The menacing deer flies were down, and the mosquitoes only came out at dusk. And even then, as a random nuisance, not in swarms like late June. Moe coasted down the hill on Brady Road toward the river, listening to the crunching of gravel under the tires of his bike, thinking back to when all his friends would ride abreast of one another; they had felt like some version of the cavalry. He thought about what his uncle had said about his sturdy arms and broad chest, looking back and forth at his shoulders and biceps as he hung onto his handlebars while going down the bumpy road. At the bottom, Moe studied Mr. Norton's house on the edge of the tree line against the hill. The horses were up near the stable, out of the sun. His pickup truck was nowhere around. *Probably at the Co-op getting feed,* Moe thought. He dragged his bike under the electric fence, rode across the corner, and dragged it under again at the other end, onto the bank of the river. He was heading to the point where TJ drowned, or sort of drowned. He was still alive, like a zombie, but not really, because zombies can move and kill you if you get too close. Moe wished he could go see TJ at the hospital. What did he look like? Were his eyes milked over like the zombies in the movies?

When Moe came up to the old bridge, he could see a shoulder poking out from behind the oak tree that he and his friends used to sit under to get out of the sun. The person had their back to him, unaware of his presence. The shoulder was familiar. The person couldn't hear him walking up and the clicking of his bike chain because of the rush and ripple of the river.

The front bike tire was the first thing that Aqua saw in the corner of his eye, and it startled him. He jerked, nearly ripping a page from the comic book he was engrossed in, and that would've been bad, because it was a nineteen sixty-five edition of Metal Men. It wasn't in mint condition, but it was in good condition.

"Whoa!" Aqua screeched as his voice uncontrollably hit a high pitch. It would've been funny to Moe, but the shock of finding Aqua sitting there was sobering.

"Hey."

"Hey," Aqua returned with a mutter, not fully collecting his voice, as he was still surprised by Moe's sudden appearance. He closed the comic book and set it on his lap.

"So, what's been going on, dude?" Moe asked unsteadily, like he was trying to coax a dog to put it on a leash.

"Ah, not too much. You?"

"Well, my Uncle Eric's staying with us while recovering from a pretty bad car accident he got into."

"Yeah, I heard."

"How'd you hear about it?" Moe asked, surprised and almost defensive.

"Regina Myers's mother works at the hospital and told my grandpa when we were picking up some stuff at the store. Grandpa told me not to tell anybody, but I guess I can tell you because it's your uncle and all."

Moe sat down crossed-legged on the mossy ground in front of Aqua. "My mom told me that he's kinda odd and that I shouldn't spend a lot of time around him. I dunno . . . he seems all right to me. My mother never talked much about him. I guess I was really little when I saw him last before we moved up here, but I don't remember him."

"What'd she mean by 'odd'?"

"She wouldn't say. She just said odd and left it at that."

"Wow, that's weird."

"I know." The boys were quiet for a moment, both picking at the clumps of moss, then Moe grinned mischievously and glance at Aqua. "So was Regina with her mom?"

Aqua smiled and blushed. "I wish."

"If she filled out more than she did last summer, I bet her boobs are like watermelons now."

The boys chuckled.

"Probably more like beach balls."

Moe, still chuckling, said, "Remember that time last year, out in the hallway in front of Mrs. Lownsberry's class, when Ry was trying to dance like Michael Jackson—"

"Oh, yeah, yeah," Aqua interrupted.

"And he spun around and accidentally slapped Regina's tit when she walked by?"

Aqua laughed louder. "Yeah, everyone froze, including Regina. Then Ry tried fixing her sweater, touching her tit again, and she smacked him." Aqua paused, trying to catch his breath between laughing so hard. "Dude, that was hilarious."

"I know, right?"

The boys laughed a little longer, picturing the event in their minds, seeing Ry's nervousness and bumbling attempt to recover. The laughter subsided like waves behind a boat slowing down to dock.

"Have you seen Ry or any of the other guys since . . . well, you know?" Moe asked, biting one side of his bottom lip.

"Ry came by just after my grandma came home from the hospital, but my grandpa told him he thought he should go home. So, he wasn't there long. Besides, my mom came up and was spending a couple days with us then, but she had to get back to work. Ry did tell me that his parents told him not to hang out with any of his old friends."

"Yeah, my mother kinda told me the same thing, but now I don't know. I'm not sure. Have you seen Creeper or Sup?"

"Nah. You?"

"Nope. No one 'cept you. Hey, you wanna go for a bike ride?"

"That'd be cool, but I gotta get back soon."

"Oh, your grandparents got ya on a short leash?"

"Nah, it's not like that. My grandma needs us to help her a lot now, and my grandpa can only do so much." Moe nodded his head that he understood, then Aqua pressed his lips together for a moment in thought. "Hey, Moe, do you . . . um . . . do you, I mean, what do think about God?"

"Whaddya mean?"

"Do you believe in God?" Aqua asked, squinting to mask his sensitivity on this particular subject.

"Sure. I mean, we're supposed to, right? Why do you ask?"

Aqua shrugged his shoulders while looking toward his feet. "I don't know, just wondering." He thought a moment longer. "It just doesn't make sense. It's sorta like these comic books, you know?"

Moe chuckled. "Yeah, can you imagine if Jesus were Mercury from *Metal Men* and they tried nailing him on the cross? He'd be like, 'Sorry, dude, that ain't gonna work.' " Moe put his arms out as if he were Jesus being crucified, made a popping sound while making a gesture of freeing each arm, then waved and struck a pose. "See ya."

Aqua smiled politely and muttered, "Yeah." He didn't press the conversation any further, knowing that it may have been a little too serious. Instead, he got up and put the comics in his pack, told Moe he had to get home, and asked if he wanted to try to meet again tomorrow. Moe agreed, and they both made their way over the bridge, under Mr. Norton's fence, and onto Brady Road. When they got to the top of the hill, the two boys heard the sirens of an ambulance off in the distance, but assumed it was a fire truck.

"I bet someone started a fire over by the campground again," Moe complained.

"Probably," Aqua replied indifferently. There was a short pause as they both listened.

"Well, I'll catch ya later, dude." Moe then jumped up on a pedal and launched himself to continue west on Bray to his house a half mile away.

"See ya." And with that, Aqua turned south on Wilson Hill Lane, which had sparsely planted summer cabins, before coming to a dead end and the path that had been a shortcut to his grandparents' since he and his friends could remember.

Halfway through the forty acres of wood that separated the end of the road and Aqua's home, he could see the flashing lights through the pine trees. At first, he thought there was a fire by his house, but as he got nearer, the white box shape of the ambulance became clear. It was backed up to the porch of his grandparents' home. He dropped his bike and backpack at the tree line and ran toward the house. Aqua's grandmother was already in the truck on the stretcher. A heavyset female was leaning over, sticking leads onto her chest, sifting her blouse this way and that to get access. There was an oxygen mask on her face. Aqua wanted to climb in, then heard his grandpa behind him on the porch, talking to the other EMT, a large man, like his partner. Grandpa was disheveled. Aqua could tell by the way he was standing, with one hand on the doorknob and the other holding onto the frame, that he was weak. The years of drinking and smoking had taken their toll way before he quit. Henry wasn't using his oxygen. Aqua ran between his grandpa and the man and grabbed a black bag on the kitchen counter. It had a small tank about eighteen inches long inside and clear rubber tubing coming out of it. He rushed it over and interrupted the men talking.

"Here, Pa, put this on."

Henry smiled unsteadily and tapped Aqua on the shoulder as if to thank him. He took the cannula first, putting it to his nose, and with hands trembling, wrapped the two thin tubes around his ears. He took a deep breath.

The EMT, catching on to the situation, grabbed one of Henry's arms. "Mr. Baltruss, I think you should probably have a seat." The man and Aqua walked Henry over to his recliner. Aqua carried the bag with the oxygen tank in it, being careful to make sure the tubing had enough slack, so it didn't get pulled from his grandfather's face. Henry's face was slowly regaining its color. The man studied him for a moment. "Mr. Baltruss, are you okay now?"

Henry nodded. "Yes, I'm fine."

"Okay, then. As I was saying, we have Sylvia stable. She's breathing on her own. If you'd like, you can ride with her to the hospital?"

"No, that's okay," Henry replied, slightly exhausted. "I don't really have anyone to follow up in a car except my grandson here. And I think his license is expired." Henry winked at Aqua. "Don't worry, I'll be all right once I catch my breath. The boy and I will drive up later."

"Okay, well, the hospital has your number if anything changes, and if you have any questions, please call. Okay?"

"Yep, yep, I got it. Thank you."

The man left, grabbing two large bags, one with a monitor, and one with other medical supplies. Aqua followed behind him and shut the door, then ran back over to his grandfather. "What happened, Pa?" he asked, but Aqua already knew the answer.

"Your grandmother had another attack, kid," Henry replied with a slight wheeze coming from his chest.

"Was it bad?" Aqua knew that was a stupid question too. The scene he had returned to clearly showed that it was.

"It doesn't look good, Arthur." Henry leaned forward in his chair and put his elbows on his knees. Still out of breath, he directed his grandson to get his keys and wallet. "I think we better head on up to the hospital. You can help me out to the car."

"Sure, Pa," Aqua said, his eyes flooded with tears. He was certain this was his fault. His grandmother was dying because of the things he and his friends had done. After she went through emergency and on to the intensive care unit, it wasn't long before Sylvia was on a ventilator. Henry kept her alive for two days before he honored the DNR order.

The funeral was on the weekend before school started. It was Labor Day weekend. This was the last big hoorah for the tourists, creating a surreal dichotomy in the town of vacationers enjoying the last days of summer, which was interrupted with a procession for a woman many cared for, and causing looks of contempt from those in sandals and holding ice cream cones. Regardless of the meeting that took place a month before in the basement of the church, all the families attended, plus the members of the church, and the quilting club. Where Henry was often grouchy and sarcastic, Sylvia had always been pleasant to everyone who knew her, quick with a smile, a greeting, a handshake, or a hug. She was never gossipy or acerbic, and only caused envy in the patterns she concocted for her quilts. She was respected for her patience and kindness.

Aqua, who was being used as a crutch and an anchor by his inconsolable and neurotic mother, was directed by his grandfather, who witnessed the unbearable burden his grandson was forced into, to go outside for a while. The funeral home sat adjacent to a parking lot overlooking the river. Just before the services began, the five friends somehow gravitated toward one another, like beads of water finding a low spot on a canvas. The low spot was behind the utility shed, hidden from view, on a slope near the bank of the river. Everyone was wearing ties except Supper, but he was wearing a black suit coat, which was why he positioned himself directly in the shade of the shed. Greetings were exchanged, followed by a chorus of "Sorry about your grandma." Aqua and Supper stood opposite one another in the lopsided circle the boys had formed, occasionally darting a scrutinizing look at the other, while Moe, Ry, and Creeper made small talk about what teachers they were getting stuck with. Then Supper surprised everyone.

"Look, Aqua . . ." The way Supper began his sentence suggested that something important was about to be said, so the other three boys instantly stopped talking. "I just want to say I'm sorry about everything that happened."

At first, no one could take their eyes off Supper, but there was too long a pause before Aqua said anything, so they all stared at him for a response. He shrugged his shoulders. It was awkward to process the apology, because to Aqua, he thought the matter was over with. Besides, Supper seemed lesser now, smaller. His mea culpa further discredited him. He was deconstructed and didn't seem worthy of Aqua's hate *or* revenge. It wasn't settled, but it was over with. Aqua had already put Supper into a category, an ambiguous category. He had to live with him; had to go to school with him; shared the same friends. Now it was as though everything was supposed to go back to the way it was before TJ drowned? Aqua couldn't convey the way he felt to anyone, because it wouldn't make a difference, and also, the feelings weren't definitive. They were just a useful tool for now to go on living. He also couldn't reason to himself why he felt a sense of pity toward Supper, but it was there.

"That's okay," Aqua replied, looking toward the ground, then leveling his eyes at Supper. "I guess there was a lot of bad stuff that happened, and we can't do anything about it now."

"Yeah, Aqua's right, man," Ry interjected with excitement, seeing the possibility that things could be the way they used to be. But Aqua's response still seemed incomplete, at least for a moment. Supper put out his hand, and the two boys shook. "This is cool, man." To Ry, it seemed they were all moving on now, a new chapter in their ongoing lives together. "I only wish TJ was okay and could be with us, too."

Creeper concurred with an unwavering, "Yeah."

Moe and Supper both nodded, as if in polite agreement, keeping their eyes toward the ground. Aqua said nothing but remained pensive. In fact, he felt a sort of vindication that he didn't want to admit to anyone. The fact that TJ had tried to kill him, and the struggle it had been to break free from his attack, was still very present for Aqua. TJ got what he deserved, he thought, but that was something he could never share with anybody.

The boys talked some more about school coming up before Aqua was yelled for by his Aunt Liz, the one with the grand piano. "There you are. Come on, Arthur, your grandpa needs your help."

CHAPTER 9

Although Eric was still in traction for most of his injuries, by the time school started, he could manage the basic functions of a daily routine, but nothing too strenuous. This, however, gave him the incentive to heal faster. But he always did heal fast, and rarely, if ever, was he sick. He could never tolerate not being in complete control of his body, so he never drank or took drugs beyond prescribed medication when necessary. He didn't like the feeling of being altered in any way. It enraged him. By now, he was annoyed by television and movies, and exhausted with all the books and magazines his nephew brought home from the library for him to read. He quit taking the pain killers, preferring instead to wrestle with the discomfort and with the need to move more. He had to get out and become more physical, and not just the occasional doctor's appointments. He pressured Karen to drive him around, and she did, but it was hardly a time for either one of them to bond. She drove him around town, around the park where they were originally supposed to meet; local spots where people fished; the best place to watch the fireworks on the fourth, and so on. He questioned a lot and made small sarcastic remarks, but nothing very clever, just usually crude, like, "Ah, so this is where the lovers first hook up and do a lot of their inbreeding." And "This must be where the retards start training for the Special Olympics." Karen paid little attention, because, so far, his snide comments had been saved for her, never James, and they were few and far between for Eric. In fact, he made pleasant but alarming comments as well. Like the time he said, "This ain't so bad. I see myself living here." But the thought of Eric living near her, and James made Karen shiver.

The start of the school year made it harder for Karen to keep track of her son. She now worked from one to nine at night. She begged for the five in the morning until the one in the afternoon, but her employer told her she didn't have the seniority yet, and it'd be unfair to the others. She encouraged James's band practice after school and his visits to the library after that, but that was only until eight o'clock, when it closed. When she caught James and Arthur hanging out together, she said nothing, and was actually relieved. This, she thought, would be another added distraction to keep him away from Eric, so to see the two throwing stones off the bridge into the river in town after the library closed was a mixed relief, but a relief, nonetheless.

Eric felt he was getting soft but refused the therapy that the physician recommended. Besides, that was nearly an impossibility because he would either have to drive the thirty-eight miles to the hospital every day of the week, which he couldn't, or have Karen chauffeur him, which would keep her from working. Instead, he took to moving around the yard with his walker while Karen and James were away at work and school. Although he had no X-rays yet to prove it, his pelvis seemed healed, or was at least at a point where he could put pressure on it. He still had two weeks before his jaw could be unwired. He had some freedom with his shoulder and was pushing himself more and more to make it mobile. And although his leg was far from being healed, he was using it to stabilize his balance every chance he got. To him, surviving the crash was further proof of how powerful he really was.

* * * * *

There was a lassitude about his grandfather now that Aqua found impenetrable at times, and it frightened him. Aqua couldn't handle the loss of his grandpa right now. He would be all alone. Although he would return to live with his mother, he felt that it would be worse than if, by some miracle—an oversight by the state—he was able to live on his own in his grandparents' house. However, it seemed as though he was now taking care of his grandfather more than the other way around, making sure he ate, took his medication, stayed on his oxygen, and washed. But Aqua had to be clever and invent ways to remind him, to make sure it didn't sound as though he were treating him like a child, as this would agitate Henry if he suspected it. Aqua would say, "Pa, I put some new towels and wash cloths out for us." Or "Pa, I'm getting myself a class of water, would you like for me to get you one too so you can take your pills?"

It was a mixed blessing that, in many ways, Henry's depression gave Aqua more freedom, but with that freedom came more responsibility; picking up groceries so his grandfather didn't have to leave the house; cleaning the house; picking up the bills at the post office and making sure they got paid; balancing the checkbook. The pharmacy even got used to Arthur coming in to pick up Henry's medicine. It started with him coming up to the window alongside his grandfather, then going to the window alone while Henry sat on the waiting bench, then seeing him wait in the car through the parking lot window, then verifying over the phone, then eventually: "Are you here to pick up your grandpa's medication, Arthur?"

"Yes, Mr. Kalchik."

The library became Aqua's bar after work. Though it was getting colder at dusk and in the evenings, there was no snow yet, so Aqua could ride his bike, and so could his friends. Creeper had loved the library ever since he picked up his first book on Houdini, and now he had an even better reason. Ry followed Moe there after band practice. And Supper was told by Creeper that everyone had been getting together there after school. It was a good excuse for the boys to give their parents. To hear all the boys, talk at home, it was the most challenging school year yet, with book reports, homework assignments, pop quizzes. All paraphrasing each other emphatically how Mr. Swanson, Ms. Maddix, and Mr. and Mrs. Klaft all liked the research done with actual books and not via the Internet, asking for page numbers, editions, and quotes. The small window when the library was open on Saturday was another occasion for the boys to get together as well.

In many ways, it was as exciting as their adventures in the summertime. They were clandestine rendezvous, like spies gathering during the Cold War in an Eastern Block café, whispering secrets to one another so other spies posing as locals wouldn't hear them. And this at the corner table in the rear of the library in a two-story brick building overlooking the bridge and river on the north end of town. It was built in nineteen hundred two.

And from then until nineteen forty-seven, it was used as the post office and town hall.

The table of spies soon became exposed, as the librarian, Lilly Henderson, mentioned seeing the dutiful boys to Ry's parents when she saw them at the Dollar Store.

"I cannot believe how much time the boys are spending at the library," Lilly bellowed. "And, oh my goodness, they are so well-behaved. I only wish more of our kids would go to the library. It's a dying institution. I'm surprised I still have a job." Lilly was always loud when she spoke, seeming only able to speak at one volume setting. She was an elderly widowed woman whose husband died two weeks after he retired from foundry work downstate. Many thought she had some sort of hearing deficit, but she was somehow aware when a person talking was becoming a distraction for other patrons in the library, though, she never approached the culprit in hushed tones. Instead, she addressed the matter in a succinct and audible manner so that everyone could hear: "Keep it down, please!"

As much as Sarah and Jim Devos had warned and pleaded with their son to stay away from his old friends, they ultimately accepted that it was inevitable, especially after Sylvia's funeral. In fact, all the parents of the boys realized it. But the thread of social familiarity and parent camaraderie that the adults once shared had been forever broken. They would all find ways to not cross one another's paths, made sure never to make eye contact, and to not attend the same functions. All the families quit attending Minister Troman's services. The Bunkers had been trying to get positions with other health organizations so they could relocate. Jim Devos applied to companies out of state. And the Arbuckles put their home up for sale and arranged that if it sold, they'd move to Minnesota and stay with family until they could get on their feet. Henry knew he would die in the place he retired, and besides, he couldn't leave Sylvia, who was buried in the town cemetery. As for Karen, she was ready to leave, but needed to get rid of Eric first. She didn't want him following her and James. She figured she could pay off her mortgage in two years, as long as she exhausted her savings. Then, with the money she got from the sale, she might be able to find a place out West, preferably California, and reinvent her and James's life.

Moe was beginning to get used to his uncle. In fact, Eric seemed to have many of the same interests as he did. And Moe was surprised to find out how much his uncle knew about modern music. It was refreshing to have someone to not only talk to about all the things he liked, but who would listen as well, and let him finish his sentences. Moe was beginning to question his mother's reason for telling him to avoid his uncle. Was it a childhood incident? A temperament that he had when they were young? Whatever the problem was, Moe couldn't see it. Moe would help Uncle Eric get around, and he was very appreciative, and more than that, appeared humbled by the help, telling him, "I don't know what I'd do without your help, James. If you weren't so strong, I'd certainly be in trouble." Moe liked showing how supportive he could be when Eric put his weight on his shoulder while he was helping him to his walker, then sliding his hand down the boy's arm to his hand to steady himself.

By mid-October it was getting cold, a cross between coats or jackets, and the five boys were far less segregated, joining one another openly in public, but all except Ry were still apprehensive about knocking on the front doors of their friends' homes. But Ry only ever came to Aqua's house unannounced. So the boys would often arrange ahead of time where and when they would get together, or in the case of Aqua and Moe, tap on each other's bedroom window.

On one Saturday morning, knowing that was the time Moe's mother did her grocery shopping, Aqua, Ry, and Creeper, who all met in the Baltrusses driveway, rode their bikes over to Moe's house. Noticing Miss Moby's car was out of the yard, Aqua rapped on Moe's window. Being a modular home with a foundation higher than most, Aqua had to reach above his head. There was no reply. Aqua and the other two boys waited and tried again. Still no reply. Ry recommended going to the door but knowing that Moe's uncle had been staying with them, Aqua and Creeper were worried about how they would be received. On the third attempt, startling Aqua, Moe yanked up the blinds. Moe opened the window.

"Hey, dudes!"

"Shit, dude! You scared me."

"Sorry, bro."

"What took you so long?"

"I was talking to my uncle," Moe answered enthusiastically. "Come on around to the front door. I want you guys to meet him. I think you'll like him. He's pretty cool. Hey, where's Sup?"

"Ah, he had to go with his mom and dad somewhere outta state this weekend," Creeper replied, disappointed.

"What about your ma? What if she comes back while we're in the house?" Aqua asked.

"Yeah, I don't think she'll be back for a while. She just left not too long ago."

The boys walked around to the front of the house, leaving their bikes out of sight. When Aqua walked in, he was surprised to see Moe's uncle setting plates on the kitchen table. Especially since the last he heard, the uncle needed to use his walker and Moe for balance. Now, although his leg was still in a cast, he was moving around on it, and both arms seemed operable. Although he seemed to favor the left one, resting it across his stomach when he wasn't using it. He was wearing a tank top, and Aqua could see some scarring plus some minor shades of bruising on his shoulder. He had a silver chain with a crucifix around his neck that looked more like the style of a rapper, as if more for show than spiritual comfort or representation. He had broad and thick shoulders, dark eyes, and thick eyebrows, like a wise guy in a mobster movie. He didn't have a belly, but wasn't tapered either—to Aqua, he seemed evenly cylindrical. He was tall, Moe, and probably even Supper (because he and Moe were about the same height) only came up to his nose, if that. His voice was coarse like Aqua's grandfather's, though deeper, or maybe just younger. It was intimidating somehow, like the voice of someone brought in for questioning in a crime show, who laughed off the good cop/bad cop routine the detectives tried to use to get a confession.

"Would all you boys like some pancakes?" Eric asked, as if not expecting any refusals.

The three boys looked at one another, as if to say, "why not?"

"Sure, Moe's uncle," Ry replied for all.

"Just call me Uncle Eric."

They all took off their coats or hoodies, hats, and gloves and threw them in a corner by the door, the way they used to.

"My uncle is celebrating getting his jaw unwired," Moe announced, slightly animated, a way Aqua hadn't seen him behave since before the killings.

"That's right, boys!" Eric shouted from over at the stove in the kitchen. "Yesterday my yap was freed from bondage! Free at last! Free at last! Thank God Almighty, my jaw is free at last!" Eric chuckled. "Have a seat, fellas. As soon as I get these flapjacks ready, James can introduce me to his motley crew." He winked at his nephew.

"Too bad Sup wasn't here," Creeper said quietly, so that only his friends standing near him could hear. "He loves pancakes."

"Dude, you gotta be brain dead not to like pancakes," Moe responded.

"Well, I guess that leaves TJ out," Ry blurted automatically, without thinking of how insensitive his statement was.

All the boys became quiet, and Ry, frozen by his own remark, could only dart his eyes around at his friends to try to anticipate their reactions. Then Creeper snickered, and the laugh became infectious.

"What's so funny over there, fellas?"

"Nothing, really, Uncle Eric. We were just joking about a friend," Moe answered.

"Hey, James," Eric added, "see what everyone wants to drink, would ya? But you know I want my juice."

Moe offered his friends a selection of orange juice, milk, or water. All chose milk, but Moe poured himself some orange juice, as well as his uncle. When the pancakes were ready, Eric placed the platter of them in the center of the table, and he asked Moe to grab the syrup and butter, then simply said, "Dig in." And they did, losing all manners after Moe and Eric set the stage by stabbing two and three pancakes at a time and reaching over one another's plates. It was friendly chaos. The movement and clanking filled the immediate absence of conversation. After the boys had savored the first few initial bites of fluffy buttermilk pancakes soaked in artificially flavored Spartan brand syrup, Eric asked his nephew for introductions.

"So, James, what are your friends' names?"

Still chewing, starting on his left side, Moe pointed with his fork and, working clockwise around the table, he began, "This is Ryan Devos, or Ry for short."

"Hello, Ry for short," Eric said, causing a few chuckles.

"Hello." Ry giggled.

Aqua was astonished. People had overheard their nicknames for one another before, and they had never told each other that it was a secret that they shouldn't tell anyone else, but no one in the group ever introduced their friend to an outsider before with the name that was earned by their friendships, and certain rites of passage. He looked to Creeper to see if he showed any signs of concern. Creeper did sit a little straighter, but Aqua couldn't determine if it was just because he was being introduced next, or if he was feeling at least some small part of the betrayal that Aqua was.

"And then there's Jake Arbuckle."

"Oh, like Fatty Arbuckle?" Eric added flippantly.

"Well, actually, he was some relation in my family tree. Like a great-great-great uncle or something."

"No shit!" Eric bellowed. "That's pretty interesting."

All the boys except Moe were surprised by the adult saying "shit" in front of them. The word wasn't surprising, but no adult had ever said it so naturally or carelessly in front of them before, as if he were their peer, their equal.

"And we call him Creeper," Ry interrupted, seemingly and instantly caught up in the same familiarity as Moe.

"Creeper?" Eric's voice rose with the question. "That's strange. How'd you get a nickname like that?"

Moe and Creeper explained back and forth and over one another the simple history of how his sister had labeled him, but Creeper then added the byline of his annoyance with his sister, and how intrusive she could be. To which Eric smiled, chuckled, and added a family friendly anecdote of his own about his sister when they were about the same age. As these exchanges were going on, Aqua wanted to disappear. He didn't want to be introduced next. He felt that if he focused on eating and kept his mouth full, when attention came to him, he'd be unable to speak. This sudden openness felt reckless and disloyal.

"And what's your nickname?" Eric asked Aqua abruptly, without warning, just winding down from the laughter. Aqua put his hand over his mouth to accentuate that it was hard to answer, and because of the pause, Moe answered for him.

"We call him Aqua. It's short for Aquaman."

"Seriously? Like from the *Aquaman* comics?"

"Yeah. He used to really love the *Aquaman* comics when we were young," Creeper interjected.

"Still does," Moe added mischievously, grinning through a mouth of pancakes.

Aqua's only defense was to respond with an unconvincing, "No, I don't." But Moe's further betrayal left Aqua feeling even more vulnerable and on the spot. *How could he*? This was a secret they kept even from their other friends.

"Pretty cool," Eric said. "What I used to like reading when I was young was Thor and Namor. They both seemed really bad-ass and didn't make any compromises."

When Aqua was eleven, he'd had this argument at school during lunch hour with Eddy Jewel. They mutually agreed that Marvel and DC Comics had their pros and cons, but when Aquaman was mentioned, Eddy called the superhero a wimp because he was always summoning sea creatures to do all his fighting for him. He had added that Namor, the Sub-Mariner, fights his own battles. "Oh, yeah, well, that's because all the animals in the sea like and respect Aquaman. That's why they help him," Aqua had blasted. "Namor is a dick, and nobody likes him!" Aqua wondered if Moe's uncle was trying to prod him or was challenging him. Aqua knew he couldn't get into a debate with him, since he was the most popular guy in the room now. Even more than that, Aqua felt this was a guy he shouldn't make enemies with. Maybe that's why his friends were being so accepting of Moe's uncle. Were they a little afraid? Was this all just a nervous response?

"So, what's your real name, Aquaman?" Aqua couldn't determine if Eric was asking out of politeness or sarcasm.

"Arthur," Aqua replied quickly, and just as quickly took another bite of pancake.

"Arthur what?"

"His name is Arthur Baltruss," Ry blurted.

After pausing for a moment, Eric asked again, "I'm sorry, Arthur, what is your last name?"

Aqua swallowed the food in his mouth and looked Eric in the eye. He looked intent. "Baltruss." Eric seemed momentarily riveted, and Aqua couldn't help but ask, "Why?"

"Oh, no reason, no reason," Eric stammered. "For a minute there I thought you said *Blatuss.* They were a family I knew downstate. But you said Baltruss. Right?"

"Yeah, that's right."

Aqua studied the man for a moment, perplexed, as he looked down to cut up his pancakes. Ry mentioned Supper and how he couldn't make it, then Creeper explained the story of how that nickname evolved. Chatter and jokes continued over breakfast, but on occasion, Aqua would notice Moe's uncle out of the corner of his eye, watching him. Creeper showed Moe's uncle some of the tricks he could do with cards, and in turn, Eric showed everyone a few of his own, party tricks he learned as a young inmate, but he didn't tell the boys that. They all finished, and Moe naturally started helping his uncle clean the table, but Eric stopped him and told his nephew to go hang out with his friends.

This was intriguing to Eric. What was his sister up to? Why did she want this young boy and his family dead? Further, why was there a *group* of people who wanted them dead? And who was this group? Eric wanted to—had to—find out more. This Arthur was certainly no threat, and it was clear he and James were good friends. Was there money involved? Property? It had to be something horrible or threatening. This was not the sister he knew. How could she have possibly been planning to have the young boy killed as well? Would James know?

Eric knew Karen wouldn't give up any more details, not now. He had to get close to this mystery, and he knew the only way to do it was through James and his friend, if not friends. He could confront Karen, even threaten her, but then she would only work harder to keep James away from him. Plus, Eric knew he was still vulnerable, and it'd probably be some time before he would be completely recovered or free from traction and all his restrictions.

* * * * *

The following Monday Supper met with his friends during lunch hour.

"We're moving to Rhinelander, Wisconsin."

"That doesn't even sound like a real place," Ry complained.

"Yeah, it sort of sounds like something out of *Lord of the Rings*," Moe said mockingly. "We shall go to Rhinelander and form an alliance with the Rhinelandeons," he added with a deeper voice to imitate some noble character.

"My dad is going to open up his own practice there."

"What about the one here in town?" Aqua asked.

"I didn't know it, but my mom and dad already sold it," Supper replied. "They sold it a while ago. My mother has just been kinda helping out until the new people take over."

"Man, this sucks balls," Ry muttered.

"That's fucked up, dude," Creeper added. "I'm not supposed to say anything, but we're probably going to be moving too."

"What!" Aqua blurted unintentionally. The others reacted the same way, but with a sigh or breath, or nonverbal grunt.

"Yeah, my dad has actually already been working downstate, and I guess the company offered him a full-time position, but it's based out of Minnesota. We have relatives out there, and I guess if we move, we'll be staying with them."

"Man, this sucks big balls," Ry yelled.

One of the teachers, Mr. Swanson, was standing a few tables away, chatting with some of the other students. He charged over to the boys' table. With a slender six-foot-six-inch frame, his Scandinavian features would have normally made him imposing, but a childhood accident had deviated his nasal septum severely, sloping his long Norwegian nose to the right of his face, putting the left nostril over the center of the philtrum. The joke had been passed down from class to class over the last fifteen years he worked at the school, to "be careful of Mr. Swanson. He can sniff out trouble anywhere, even around corners."

"Mr. Devos, what did you just say?" Mr. Swanson demanded.

"We were just saying how the Wings would do better this year if instead of using pucks, that they used big balls, Mr. Swanson," Supper interrupted. Girls sitting at a table next to the boys giggled.

"I am not talking to you, Mr. Bunker," the teacher said firmly. "I am speaking to Mr. Devos." Keeping his gaze on Supper, he slowly turned to Ry, expecting an answer.

"Yes, sir, that's right," Ry agreed, sliding his elbows off the table and leaning back in his chair, as if to display some form of respect.

Mr. Swanson glared at Ry a moment longer. "You need to watch your mouth, young man. Next time, I'm not going to let your friends make excuses for you. Is that understood?" Ry nodded quickly. Then Mr. Swanson walked away slowly with a deliberation that appeared less intimidating than it was intended to, and more like a bad imitation of someone trying to do so.

"Geez, what got his nose outta joint?" Supper mumbled so only his friends could hear. And with that, no one could help but let out a short burst of laughter. Mr. Swanson turned around quickly and gave the boys a hard look. They quieted, looking either down at the table or away. Then Mr. Swanson slowly continued meandering through the cafeteria. The boys went on to chuckle amongst themselves.

Aqua was impressed by Supper. It was like the old days, he thought, before all the bad stuff happened. He almost felt like they were a team again. He was even missing seeing TJ there. It was nice to have that comradeship. At home, it was so depressing. He loved his grandpa dearly, but with his grandma gone, it seemed as though she had taken a part of him with her, the best part. He was starting to take care of himself a little better, but that was all there was. Grandpa was like a low-grade functioning robot to Aqua, and although he tried, he didn't know what conversations to have to make him interested.

Creeper told everyone they should come over the weekend after next because his mother and sister would be downstate visiting their dad, who had contracted some work, and the only reason they were leaving him home alone was because they didn't want to take the dogs and had no one to watch them. Creeper's father and mother both warned him that he wasn't to allow any friends over, and there would be "dire consequences" if he did. The boys all agreed to show up, and Supper added that he'd have the house to himself shortly after on the weekend of opening day for deer season, because his parents would be in Wisconsin, so they all could get together then too. Moe liked the timing as well because his mother was filling in for one of the ladies at work, since the lady liked to hunt with her husband, and had the eleven to eight in the morning shift. This meant she would be sleeping in till late in the afternoon the following day, giving him the freedom to stay up with his friends and sleep in late as well.

CHAPTER 10

During the day, while Eric was alone, he snooped ardently to find clues to why his sister and, by her own word, a group of others wanted some small-town hicks killed. A child and his grandparents no less. What sort of threat could they possibly be? If anybody here had a few thousand dollars to put someone down, it would have to be for a very good reason. What secret was Karen hiding? Better still, how would the death of this family benefit his sister? Karen wasn't an irrational person. The thing she valued the most was James. That had to be the only reason she'd risk everything. And what about the "group?" Could it be the same thing motivating them—their kids? Eric had been in James's room before, because he fantasized about him, but now, he was looking for something, anything, that would lead to a theory, a hypothesis.

Eric sat on the floor of the bedroom, still unable to bend his right leg because of the cast. He put his back against the bed. He thought about when he was a kid. Where did he hide things? He grinned, pulled back the bed cover, and slid an arm between the box spring and mattress and felt paper. He pulled it out, expecting to see a playboy centerfold, but instead, he found pictures of boy bands. There was Simple Plan, Good Charlotte, Nsync. "What the fuck is this?" Eric said to himself. "Is my nephew a goddamn faggot?" Eric hadn't really expected to find anything incriminating when reaching under the mattress, other than boyhood indiscretions, but this made him even more curious. "There has to be a pinup somewhere." He reached again, farther toward the center of the bed, and this time, he touched the binding of a book. "A diary? I don't fucking believe it," he mused to himself. "This kid really is a fucking faggot."

The first few pages were about Aqua, the first having been written three years earlier, when Moe was in the sixth grade. It was crude but revealing. This was not the smoking gun that Eric was looking for, but it gave him a unique window into his nephew's mind. Better yet, his soul. He now knew more than Karen did about her son, and he relished it. Her son had feelings for other boys, he was confused, and he prayed to God that this would change. It was a sporadic diary, week by week on the average, sometimes spanning a month, and half pages mostly. Then Eric finally came across an entry for June eleventh, a little over four months prior, and noticed immediately the lengthy writing:

I don't know if what my friends and I did today was right or wrong, but we should know at church on Sunday. What Sup says makes perfect sense, but still, I'm worried . . .

The more Eric read, the louder and louder he became. He caught himself and stopped, looking up and around. He got to his feet and pivoted his way through the house, peering out the windows and doors to see if anybody was outside near the house and may have overheard him. Eric felt as though he had just discovered classified information. When he knew that it was clear, he said, "Oh my God!" like a gold miner shouting "Eureka!" He put one hand over his mouth and held the book out in front of him with the other in disbelief, not reading any more at the moment, but taking in the sight of it, as if to verify the reality. He sat down on his bed in the living room, first looking out the front window to make sure no one had pulled in the yard while he was distracted. Then he continued to read. Every murder was written down, the initial apprehension, the coercion by Supper, or "Sup," the division in the group over Aqua, and even TJ's drowning, followed by the parents' discovery of what the boys had been doing, and the meeting the boys couldn't hear in the basement of the church. Eric was trembling with excitement. He hobbled into the bathroom and started to jerk off in the sink, but his breathing was still labored because of the broken ribs and the lung that, though on the mend, was still causing a sharp pain. It took away from his excitement, and he couldn't finish. He wanted desperately to feel that release, but he was too exhausted now. He slumped his way back into the living room and sat down.

He collected himself and thought, long and hard. "That's it. That's gotta be it," Eric said aloud, as though he were hashing over the details of an investigation with a partner. "There was a chance that kid Arthur and his family were going to the authorities. That makes perfect sense." Eric chuckled. "Wow, all these twisted little fuckers got away with murder. Now I've got the Holy Grail." He was quiet for a while, thinking, a myriad of thoughts and possibilities rushing through his mind. "I can get so much more money from these morons. The Baltrusses are out of the question, though. Bribing them would be useless. But the others . . . Goddamn it!" Eric shouted enthusiastically. He slapped the journal on his good leg several times. "Oh, man, I can do soooo many things with this!" Then he paused and realized that he still had to get back in good health. He still had his cast, which he wasn't due to have removed for another week, and there was still his lung and ribs as well. He knew he had to hold out until he was strong. But knowing what he knew now, he had the motivation and endurance to wait. "The fact that all this happened is not going to change." He laughed. He had to put the diary back so it wouldn't be discovered missing.

* * * * *

When Aqua got home the same day Eric found his nephew's journal, he found his grandfather slightly more animated and energetic than he had been in recent days, and even weeks. He was rummaging through two safety boxes he had set on the kitchen table.

"Whaddya doing, Pa?" Aqua asked skeptically after shutting the front door.

"Oh, just looking through some paperwork your grandmother and I put in one of these boxes years ago," Henry replied without looking up, then added, "Ah, here they are," when he found an overstuffed envelope. The envelope was filled with savings bonds that Sylvia had collected over the years.

"What is that?" Aqua pried.

"Oh, just something that was set aside for a rainy day." Henry seemed a little detached, and Aqua couldn't help feeling a little disappointed that his grandfather was being so vague. Nonetheless, Aqua asked what he'd been asking nearly every afternoon since his grandmother passed; a question not raised just for practical reasons, but one that he hoped would begin a longer conversation, like they'd had in the days when Henry wanted to hear about what Aqua did at school, or the adventures he had with his friends.

"What do you want for dinner, Pa?"

"Tonight, kid, dinner is on me. How about we get cleaned up and go to the Bait Pile?" The Bait Pile was a restaurant in the center of town that took its name from a common deer season practice, to draw in more sportsmen and outsiders. It also hosted an annual Buck Pole contest.

"Ah . . . sure," Aqua replied, surprised. Hearing his grandfather ask that sounded foreign, not at all like his grandfather had been since that evening in the basement of the church.

In the back of the parking lot, by the tree row that separated a line of lakehouses from the restaurant, the A-frame mounting stands were already lined up in preparation for opening day of deer season in three weeks, at which time they would be layered diagonally, taking up the south side of the business parking. Every time he saw the buck poles, Aqua always thought that the restaurant could use the frames for swing sets during the rest of the year, when they weren't used for displaying deer. Across the street, above the barber shop and insurance agency, lived the owners, Pat and Joe Bachelder. They owned that building as well and rented the lower floor. As soon as deer season was over, immediately following Thanksgiving, the Bachelders always moved to their home in Arizona until Memorial Day, leaving the businesses to be managed by their son and daughter-in-law in their absence.

It was a slow night, as Mondays and Tuesdays always were. The interior of the restaurant was decorated to look like an old hunting cabin, adorned with antler chandeliers, deer hoof coat racks, and black-and-white photographs of residents and sportsmen long since passed, standing proudly alongside the deer they had shot, or sturgeon they speared.

Henry and his grandson were seated at a four-patron table and waited on by Eddy Jewel's mother. Henry set his bag on the seat beside him and adjusted his tubing and cannula so it would be out of his way while he ate and drank. He put his elbows on the table and cupped his hands together as he studied his grandson sitting opposite him. At first Aqua paid no attention, too busy looking around the restaurant to see if there was anybody he knew but catching a glimpse of his grandfather's squinted stare not once, but twice, he was compelled to ask about it.

"Is there something wrong, Pa?"

There was a long, unflinching pause as Henry seemed to be thinking intently before answering.

"What would you think about leaving school for a little while?"

Aqua replied slowly and cautiously, "Whaddya mean, Pa?"

"Oh, I don't know. Maybe we could go on a little vacation."

"Where to?"

Henry started moving his hands a little when he spoke, as if uneasy about the conversation. "I was thinking somewhere out West."

"Do you mean like the west side of the state, or West-West, like California or something?"

"Yeah, West-West, but I thought New Mexico or Arizona."

Aqua shrugged his shoulders. "Sure, Pa. That sounds okay with me. When do you want to go?"

"I was thinking pretty soon, kid." Henry looked down at his hands and rubbed his palms together. "Pretty soon," he repeated in a softer voice.

Aqua watched his grandfather carefully as they got their drinks. Sensing this, Henry made no eye contact and looked out the window, talking about the strange weather patterns—rainy one day, freezing the next, then sunny and sixty degrees the day after that—almost building a case for the vacation. Aqua was curious about the trip. It seemed almost irresponsible of Grandpa, and he thought there may be a motive behind his decision, one that he'd rather not talk about. Then Aqua speculated that it may have something to do with him—perhaps what he and his friends had done—so he decided not to ask any more questions. There was no way he could know that Henry was struggling to find a way to tell his nearly fourteen-year-old grandson that he'd be lucky to have six more months to live. And that only three, maybe four, of those would be of any quality. The cancer from his left lung was metastasizing to other parts of his body. He had been given the option of surgery but given his age and the uncertain transformation of the disease, the odds were not in his favor. Chemotherapy offered even more uncertainty. And radiation treatment meant he'd have to rely on one of his daughters to take him back and forth for treatments. But given Arthur's mother's instability, the challenge would be too much for anyone to bear; plus, there was still no guarantee that they could isolate the radiation shots precisely. With that in mind, and knowing his other daughter was just starting her career and becoming very successful, feeling that the burden placed on her would be unfair, Henry knew he was at an impasse.

* * * * *

These were all the things Henry had known of before Sylvia died, but now, he had no choice but to figure out a way to deal with it.

As soon as his cast was removed, Eric felt as though he had been given a tremendous freedom. He compared it to his release from prison as he was driving back home with his sister. The analogy was an uncomfortable one for Karen. Eric seemed *too* excited, and he insisted on driving home from the hospital. Perhaps this meant he would leave soon—she could only hope. The medical equipment company had picked up the bed a few days prior, and Eric was using Karen's bedroom, while Karen slept in Moe's room, knowing he would rather his mother sleep in there because she would be less inclined to mess with his things. Moe slept on the couch mostly, but in his own bedroom when his mother wasn't home. Karen's demanding errands during the workday forced her to switch shifts with some of her coworkers, causing a great deal more stress than she already had, and she was losing even more sleep. So when Eric asked to borrow the car to go out for a bit, although she had some apprehension, the time home alone sounded so alluring, the opportunity to take a nap, outweighed her fears. In fact, she found herself hoping that James would even meet up with his friends after school at the library.

Eric drove thirty miles to the Northern Lakeside Bar & Grill and had a steak dinner with money he had lifted from his sister's purse; a dollar here, two dollars there, over the course of nearly two months, added up to a good meal. Eric felt impervious, invincible. No one could defeat him now. He was going to get what he wanted out of these worthless Podunks. After all, they were the ones who got him into this mess. They deserved to pay.

* * * * *

Because the time had switched to Daylight Savings, the days were much shorter, getting dark earlier, so at the time Supper pulled into Moe's driveway with the quad he got for his birthday a year earlier, Eric couldn't determine what the noise and glaring light were. It was six o'clock, and he was watching the news. Eric turned on the porch light and opened the door just as Supper shut the engine off, now parked on the brown lawn, and hopped off the ORV. He put his helmet on the seat, and before he could say anything, Eric spoke.

"Are you one of James's friends?"

"Yeah, I'm Gary." Supper walked up the steps and held his hand out to shake.

Eric realized then that this was the boy everyone called Supper, and also the one in the diary who'd had all the other boys believing that they'd become more powerful the more lives they took. He squeezed a little harder than normal, surprising Supper for a moment. "Well, hello there, Gary, you must be the one they call Supper?"

"Er, ah . . . yeah." Supper smiled politely, though skeptically, wondering how this guy knew his nickname. To a lot of adults, Supper could be a little off-putting, mainly because he looked arrogant and often projected a laissez-faire attitude toward adults, and that was mostly due to the fact that, up until recently, his parents often indicated the same toward him.

"Come on in here, fella, and have a seat."

Before he walked onto the carpet, Supper took his shoes off. This surprised Eric at first, then he realized it must be because Karen had conditioned the boy to do so over the years, just like the others. He did leave his jacket on, however, and sat down on the couch nearest the door. Eric stayed by the door for a moment, staring at Supper, until the boy sensed the man looking at him. He then looked up.

"Um, is James here?"

"He and his mother stepped out to get something. They should be back soon." That wasn't true. In truth, Karen had forgotten about James's dentist appointment, one that, if she didn't take him to, they would charge her a rescheduling fee. Especially with the extended hours that the practiced offered for families that can't make the normal nine to five. In the rush, James even forgot to tell his uncle that a friend may be stopping by. They left barely fifteen minutes before Supper arrived. The appointment was at six thirty, and the office was thirty minutes away. "Would you like something to drink while you wait?"

"No, thank you."

Supper was rakish and a little taller than Moe. But what Eric found even more appealing was his straight, ginger, shoulder-length hair. That was remarkable to Eric, who had envisioned a town full of hicks all having crew cuts. Or if not crew cuts, heads shaved like skinheads.

"So, what are you young dudes up to tonight?" Eric walked over and sat down at the other end of the couch, and Supper, growing more uncomfortable, wondered why he hadn't sat over on one of the chairs.

"Not much. Just plan on playing some video games . . . that kinda stuff."

"You guys gettin' together with any girls?" Eric asked with a sly grin. And before Supper could reply, Eric added teasingly, "Come on, I was your age once."

"Nah. We're just gonna stream some games," Supper replied, a little embarrassed.

Eric started breathing faintly heavier as his heart rate climbed. The thought of what this boy could do for him made him excited. But he had to take it slow, suppress his urges so the boy wouldn't run.

"So you don't care for the girls?" Eric tried asking in a way that showed no judgment, but the tone was awkward, clumsy even.

Supper fidgeted and shifted in his seat uncomfortably. "No, I mean, yeah, I care for the girls. It's just we're going to get together and play games. You know? Just hanging out and stuff. Maybe eat some pizza."

"Uh-huh. So, you all been friends for a long time?" Eric knew the answer. He was still trying to stall; trying to think of the right questions and filling the time before he could pitch what he really wanted.

"Since preschool. We all met in preschool." He nodded longer than necessary. "Yep."

"What else do you guys do for fun around here?"

"Just the normal things, I guess."

"Like what?"

"Ah, I don't know. I imagine the same things you did when you were young." Supper was finding it hard to read Moe's uncle. Was he being genuinely friendly, just making conversation? Or was he fishing for something?

"Well, I did a lot of things when I was young." Eric's eyes followed the contour of Supper's body from head to toe, imagining him without his coat. "I loved baseball. Used to go to a park near where we lived. You could always jump into a pickup game. Didn't have many video games, but I loved pinball. There were some electronic games, but my parents couldn't afford that kind of crap. When I was about your age, we'd wait for delivery trucks delivering beer or soda to pull up outside a convenient store, liquor store, or grocery store, and when the driver took in a dolly full of beverages, we'd run up and lift a case of whatever we could grab the quickest and run off with it."

"Really?"

"Really."

"Even beer?"

"Yeah, even beer. I never drank alcohol, though, but usually the assholes I hung around with did. I just liked to see what I could get away with. You guys ever do anything like that?"

"You mean like steal stuff?" Supper asked unsuspectingly.

"Yeah, or do something else you know you're not supposed to, just to see if you can get away with it?"

Supper felt the question was less part of a conversation and more an expectation, but he reasoned that the chance that Moe's uncle could know anything about what the boys had done was very thin. "Nah, not really. It's pretty boring around here."

"It's pretty boring around here, is it?"

"Yeah, pretty much." Supper felt that the last comment was insinuating but was hoping he misinterpreted. He wanted to leave and tried thinking of an excuse to do so, but also thought it'd look too suspicious at this point.

"You know, when I was about your age, maybe one or two years older, I was put in prison."

Supper's eyes widened, and he couldn't help but show surprise. Eric noticed this and was thrilled at the response. He had his segue and knew he was getting closer to what he wanted.

Eric continued, "Yeah, dude. You see, James's—or I mean Moe's—mother and I had a real fucker of an old man. Used to beat the shit out of me and my mom. Not so much my sister, but he'd intimidate the hell out of her. So, one day I got tired of it, grabbed my Louisville Slugger, and bashed his head in. Fucking squashed it like a melon."

Supper looked as though he had stopped breathing, his mind racing and trying to process what this man was saying to him. *Is this a bad joke? Why is he telling me this?* He was finally able to put together a sentence, but the only thing that came to mind was innocuous enough but could reveal something more. "Does Moe know about this?"

"No. I imagine his mother never told him," Eric replied leeringly.

"How many years did you get?"

"Five, total. And that's because I was given leniency because of the circumstances. You know, because of my dad being an abusive prick and all." There was a pause, then Eric continued sardonically, "So did you ever do anything like that, Gary?"

"What do you mean? Like what? Like kill my dad? No, I could never do anything like that," Supper answered, embarrassingly naïve. A disturbing malaise came over him, and Eric was starting to get impatient.

"No, I think you know what I mean. Did you ever kill anyone?" Eric demanded with a stern and quiet reserve.

Supper felt paralyzed with fear, but he also knew he had to remove himself from the situation. He stood up and, breaking eye contact, simultaneously said, "I gotta go." He fumbled to try to get his shoes on without using his hand.

"Wait a minute. Not so fast there, fella." Eric stood up, taking a couple steps toward the boy.

Supper crouched down to try to pull the back of his shoe over his heel, but his tennis shoes had been tied too tight when he pried them off. His hands were shaking, and his fingers felt weak, like useless appendages. He tried desperately to untie the knot but couldn't. He thought about just putting the shoes in his hands and making a quick exit out the door in his stocking feet, possibly even leaving his quad behind because he knew he probably couldn't get it started before Moe's uncle grabbed him. Then he felt the hand on his shoulder. He jumped.

"Whoa! Easy there. Calm down, big guy." Eric pulled gently on Supper's coat. "Why don't we just sit back down on the couch and finish our conversation like adults? Trust me when I say it's in your best interest."

Supper let Eric move him back onto the couch, like a director for a school play positioning actors during rehearsal. Supper looked up into his face and stared into his eyes as if this would tell him everything he needed to know, or maybe what his next move would be. Eric sat closer to Supper than he was before, with little more than a foot between them. "Okay, here's what I know: you and your friends did some bad things, and you were sort of the ringleader. That's fine by me. Who am I to judge?" He smirked menacingly. "But the problem is, the rest of the world don't see it as simple adolescent pranks. The world knows what I did, and I paid for it. You guys, on the other hand, as far as I know, answered to no one, except for maybe Mommy and Daddy—"

Trembling, his voice shaky, Supper was barely able to interrupt, but he did. "I don't know wha-what you're talking about."

Eric chuckled. "Really? Do me a favor, then. Why don't you pull up your shirt and show me the burn marks on your back." Eric widened his eyes and dropped his jaw to mock the boy, as if anticipating his response. "Do you know what I'm talking about now?" Eric smiled, relishing the power and control he now had over this smug teenage boy. "I paid my dues for what I did. In two ways, actually. First, just by being incarcerated, and the second by what they do to you in there." Tears were beginning to well in Supper's eyes. "I really don't want to see a good-looking boy like you go to prison, and probably your parents too. After all, I think the way you tricked your friends, and the way you pulled off the murders was pretty brilliant. So . . ." Eric rested his hand on Supper's shoulder. "I think maybe you and I can work something out. Let's say I give you a chance to pay your debt free and clear. And I'll keep this as a secret just between you and me." Eric raised his eyebrows. "Hmm?"

"What do you want me to do?" Supper's voice cracked, and he had a feeling he already knew what this man was going to ask him.

"Well, I thought you and I could go over into the bedroom, get comfortable, and you could do a few things for me. No questions asked. And when it's over, it's over. As far as you're concerned, your debt is paid. Then you can go about the rest of your life like nothing ever happened. How's that?"

Tears were filling up and spilling over his eyelids and down his cheeks. Supper wanted to ask Eric how he knew about everything, but it didn't matter. He also knew, for some reason, call it instinct, maybe, that he couldn't plea or beg his way out of this. Maybe Moe's uncle was right, he had to pay his debts. He could barely nod in agreement. Eric then helped the boy stand up. Still trembling, he felt lightheaded.

"Let's take that coat off first, okay?" Eric said, unzipping it for him, then laying it on the couch. Eric put his hand onto the small of Supper's back to lead him toward Moe's bedroom. He could feel the boy shaking, and it excited him even more. Supper felt woozy, and he started leaning forward and put his hand over his mouth. Eric knew what was happening and pushed Supper toward the bathroom across the hall from the bedroom. By the time they got into the bathroom, Supper had already spit some vomit through his fingers. He then fell down to his knees over the toilet and threw up what looked like everything that could have possibly been in his stomach. "Jesus fucking Christ!" Eric snapped bitterly. "Just like a little bitch!" Supper heaved again. Eric pulled the boy's hair back. "Don't get that shit in your fucking hair." When Supper was done, Eric was still looking at him in disgust. "Start cleaning this fucking mess up and wash your face and hands." His words were landing harder and harder, like verbal punches. "I'll go get some paper towels." Eric stepped out and went to the kitchen. When he returned, he shoved the towels at Supper. "You're not getting out of this that easy. Wash up, and I want you to clean your mouth out too. Use James's toothbrush there." He pointed to the red brush hanging out of the soap dish. "There's some Listerine in the cabinet. Make sure you use it. If you're going to put that mouth on me, I don't want it smelling like goddamn vomit." Eric walked out and back in again. This time he had two pills and a glass of water. "Here, take these."

"What is it?'

"They prescribed them to me out of the hospital. It'll help you relax." Supper took the pills while Eric watched. Grabbing the boy by the hair violently, he turned him to look into his face. "Open your mouth," Eric demanded. Supper did, and Eric inspected carefully to make sure he had swallowed the pills.

Before Supper finished up in the bathroom, he found the courage to ask Eric how he discovered what they did.

"All I can tell you is that my nephew loves to write," Eric replied with a grin. Eric then led the boy into the bedroom.

CHAPTER 11

"Has anyone heard from Sup?" Creeper asked.

It was the Friday night they were all getting together at Creeper's house. His parents were away, and all the other boys had made arrangements to come over. The parents acquiesced, knowing that it was impossible to sever contact when they all lived in such a small town.

"Yeah, he was supposed to pick me up at my house," Moe added. "When me and my mom got back from the dentist, we thought we saw him on his quad ridin' down the road, but my uncle said he hadn't been over. So, it must've been someone else. I tried calling his cell phone, but no one answered." Supper was the only one who had his own cell phone.

"Why don't we try calling him again?" Ry proposed.

Moe, Ry, Creeper, and Aqua all huddled around the phone in the den, leaning in with one ear so they all could hear, but it never went to ring, instead going directly to voicemail. Aqua suggested going over to his house, but no one wanted to confront his parents yet, even Creeper, who was closest to Supper. They also thought about calling his home phone, to see if Supper would pick up. But again, they didn't want to have to talk to his parents.

"Let's go over to his house and hang out in the woods. If we see him come out or by a window, we'll get his attention and ask him what's up," Moe suggested.

Aqua shook his head. "I think Sups probably has a good reason for not being here. For one, he would've called us already. And two, we all just talked about it this morning at school."

"Yeah, but you know what, dudes?" Ry interjected with urgency. "Maybe he flipped his quad on the path in the woods and is lying there hurt right now!"

Moe waved his finger as if inspired. "I think Ry might be right. It's not like Sup to blow us off like this. I think we should check, dudes."

With that, the boys grabbed flashlights and walked through the full light to Moe's house, then the path they knew Supper would take from his house. They found fresh tire marks on a sandy two-track, but there were several other people who used quads as well, like Warren O'Dell, who lost his driver's license to DUIs but still had to make his way into town to get his case of Hamm's beer. When they made their way up to the Bunkers' house, the only light that appeared to be on was the living room light on the first floor. Through the thin drapes, the boys could make out only Mr. Bunker on the recliner and Mrs. Bunker lying back on the couch watching television. Their black lab was lying on the floor, but no Supper. There was no snow blanketing the ground that evening, for which the boys were grateful. as they didn't leave any footprints. They cautiously walked around the house to see if there were any other lights or indication of Supper's presence, but they couldn't find any. However, off the side of the attached garage was an awning that Supper kept his quad, dirt bike, and his parents kept their snowmobiles under. What the boys discovered was that the quad was still warm, and there were fresh skid marks on the ground. And they could tell this by the dirt sprayed on the fallen leaves. When the boys started to discuss their theories, unintentionally raising their voices, the Bunkers' dog started barking in the house, so the boys made a hasty retreat back to Creeper's. A pack of coyotes were yelping off in the distance on the high ground above the swamp, probably having run down and caught a wild turkey. But what they couldn't agree on is what happened to their friend. Their speculations ran wild, but they all assumed he was home by the evidence of the warm quad.

The following day, the four boys, each in his own way, tried to get a hold of Supper, but with no success. When Monday came and Supper didn't show up for school, the friends became very worried. They met in the library after school and decided to stakeout Supper's house again. This time, they would be staying among the trees and spying with binoculars.

"Maybe he's just really sick," Aqua suggested.

That didn't seem plausible to Creeper. "I bet his parents already moved him to Rhinelander."

"No way, dude," Moe challenged. "His parents wouldn't send him there to live on his own until they moved."

"Not unless maybe, he's staying with family," Ry added.

The boys sat on a huge ash deadfall thirty feet inside the tree line, where they had a decent view of the living room and Supper's bedroom, which was on the second floor, just above the living room. There was a light on in the bedroom, but that didn't mean anything. The blinds were down, and no shadows could be seen. Mr. Bunker wasn't home yet, and Mrs. Bunker was the only one they saw, moving back and forth from the living room to the kitchen, which the boys could see part of through the living room. From the stairway to the upstairs, which connected into the living room, Supper slowly came into view, wearing pajamas and slippers. He shuffled through the living room and stood beside his mother at the kitchen sink. Ry was looking through the binoculars at the time, but everyone could easily make out the extra figure.

"There he is," Ry nearly shouted with excitement.

"See, I told you guys he was probably just sick or something," Aqua said. "He probably has the flu. There's a few kids out sick at school because of it."

They all took turns looking through the binoculars, as if to verify he was all right, or just to see their old friend, so they could determine through body language what was really wrong with him. When Aqua looked, he noticed Supper leaning into his mother and her putting her arm around him. It was something he kept to himself, but it seemed peculiar. Supper, in all the years Aqua had known him, had never shown affection toward either one of his parents. And Aqua had seen him sick many times. It looked out of place to Aqua, but his other three friends concluded that the mystery had been solved. Supper was at home, already in his pajamas, getting comforted by his mother. That's why he didn't show up Friday night. Aqua expressed later, to Moe, that it still didn't make any sense, because Supper seemed perfectly healthy during the day at school that Friday. Moe agreed it was odd, but added he had gotten sick once, and it seemed to creep up in a matter of a couple hours.

When Tuesday came, there was still no sign of Supper, and as usual, the other boys met at the library after school. They could only assume their friend was very ill, and they talked about other things. Aqua mentioned that he and his grandpa were going to take a trip but had no details and thought it'd probably be around Christmas vacation, because that was the only thing that made sense. Creeper said it was "For real" now that his family was moving, although not until the week before Christmas and New Year's. Ry didn't know of any plans that his family had, but they were always talking in whispers when he came in the room, so he thought they were up to something. And Moe talked about how obnoxious and weird his uncle had been over the last few days.

"Whaddya mean?" Ry asked.

Moe shrugged. "I dunno. He just seems like he's being kind of an ass. Like hogging the TV, telling my mom we're out of orange juice, and telling her to pick some up, but not asking or saying please. And just being really sarcastic. I wish my mom would just tell him to leave. Besides, I want my bedroom back."

"Well, isn't he still recovering from his accident?" Aqua asked.

"Nah, I don't think so. He seems fine to me. I think he's just free loading like that one guy who dated my mom a few years back. More than that, he's just getting really creepy."

"Hey, I take exception to that," Creeper said, smiling and trying to make a joke.

Ry chuckled. "Oh, I get it."

"Creepy like how, dude?" Aqua asked.

"Well, like just last night. I woke up. It was the middle of the night, and he was standing between the couch and TV. It was kinda dark, so I couldn't see him that good, but he had his hands by his crotch, and when I asked, 'Is that you, Uncle Eric?' he moved away real fast into the kitchen, and said, 'Yeah, just getting some orange juice.'"

"You think he was playing with himself?" Creeper winced.

"I dunno, I couldn't tell. But just before my mom got home after I got back from the library yesterday, he said I had a nice butt for a dude."

"Whoa, what the fuck, dude?" Ry spoke a little louder than he intended to. The librarian poked her head out from her office, and all the boys dropped their eyes to the books they always kept on the table for props.

There were several other students from school in the library, and it was hard for her to pinpoint where the noise came from, so she ducked her head back in the room, but not without giving anybody who made eye contact with her a stern glare. "Man, I'd watch yourself. Maybe put up a trip wire or something."

"He didn't seem gay to me," Creeper said.

With that, it suddenly dawned on Moe that his journal was not in a safe place. If his uncle found it, the ramifications could be devastating. He had to hurry home. When Moe got home, his uncle was where he normally was, on the couch watching the news. He quickly kicked off his Mucks and dropped his book bag on the floor.

"Hey, little big man," Eric greeted.

"Hey," Moe acknowledged, then rushed toward his bedroom.

"Where you going so fast?" Eric asked.

"Just have to get something out of my bedroom."

"Like what?"

Moe, now already in his bedroom, was surprised his uncle had asked that. "Oh, just looking for one of my books for school, and forgot where I put it. That's all." Moe quickly crouched down and felt between his mattresses to see if his journal was still there. It was, so part of his panic was put to rest, but it wasn't in the general area he last remembered putting it. If his mother had found it, that would be bad enough, but if his uncle found it, his life and everybody else's would be ruined. He was sure of that. He stuck it in the liner inside his coat and quickly folded up the posters of boy bands he had collected and did the same with those.

"Did you find it?" Eric shouted.

"Nah! It must still be at school in my locker!" Moe stood up, composed himself, and walked out of the room in an unsuspecting way, headed back into the living room.

"So, you didn't find the book at school either?"

"No, maybe I just didn't look good enough."

"Well, what book did you lose?"

Moe had to think of something quick. So, he announced the first thing that came to mind as he rounded the corner into the kitchen. "Ah, just my algebra book." Moe could hear an unzipping and froze. Before Eric said anything, Moe knew his uncle had gotten into his book bag.

"You mean this algebra book?" Eric announced from the living room.

Moe's heart raced. He knew he had to step back around the corner and act surprised and not draw suspicion, but why was his uncle being so inquisitive? "You're kidding me? Where'd you find it?"

Eric was holding the book up. "Well, golly gee, it was in your book bag the whole time."

"Man, I must've really had a brain fart or something." Moe felt his face flushing.

"Or your brain just shit itself."

With a false laugh, Moe replied, "Yeah, that's a funny one, Uncle Eric."

"Yeah, the joke's on you." Eric tossed the book on top of the backpack and leaned back into the couch. Moe turned back into the kitchen behind the wall so Eric couldn't see him. "Oh, by the way, your ma called. Said she's going to be a little late."

Moe froze and muttered under his breath, "Great." He tried to think of some place to stash his journal until he could get back to it. "Oh, okay!" He tried being quiet and opened cupboard doors, trying to figure which one was used the least.

"So, what you doin'?" Eric asked.

Moe jumped, not realizing his uncle had stepped around the partition and was watching him. "Ah, nothing, was just looking for something to eat."

"Where the pots and pans are? That's a little odd."

"I guess I don't really know what I want," Moe replied weakly.

"Well, you're awfully jumpy." Eric took a couple steps toward Moe and leaned against the counter with his hip by the fridge and crossed his legs. Moe was next to the counter on the opposite side of the kitchen, which only put six or seven feet between them. "I think I know what you want, or better still, what you need." Eric had a deadpan look about him.

Moe tried processing what Eric was saying, but it was awkward. "What do I need?" Moe nervously replied, while tugging on one of the drawstrings for his hoodie.

"Yeah, at your age, you have all these hormones bouncing around, and you really don't know what to do about it, how to release it." Eric paused, and Moe couldn't determine if he was supposed to answer or not. But then Eric continued as though he was in a trance, and it didn't matter if

Moe spoke or not. "You know, a lot of young men your age have already lost their virginity." Eric seemed to be enunciating words in his sentences unevenly, almost like an alien creature trying to sound human. "And it's perfectly natural. Some people reach their sexual maturity earlier than others. So, they experiment earlier."

"I don't know what you mean," was the only response Moe could think of.

"Look, I know you like other boys. And I was just thinking that . . ." Eric was interrupted by a knock at the door. Unfazed and looking calmly over his shoulder, he replied, "Hmm, I wonder who that could be." Eric walked to the door with Moe close behind him. When he opened it, Aqua was standing on the porch, and Ry was kicking a pebble around on the concrete walk attached to the driveway. "Hey, looky here, if it isn't the Mariner, or, I mean Aquaman," Eric said tauntingly. "Oh, and it looks like one of your other partners in crime is here as well—Ry."

"Hi, sir," Aqua said as politely as he could muster. "I was just wondering if James could come over and give us a hand pushing my grandpa's truck into the pole barn? It won't start, and he needs to work on it."

"Yeah, dude. No problem," Moe interrupted hastily.

Moe slipped on his boots, stepped around his uncle, and was about to go out the door when his uncle grabbed his arm tightly, causing Moe to freeze in surprise by the strength in his uncle's grip, "I think you need to be real careful, okay?" Eric whispered in a furtive manner.

"Yeah, I will," Moe answered timidly, unsure of what the sentence implied, whether it was to be careful moving the pickup, or in reference to the conversation they had been having, like a warning to keep his mouth shut. Moe was sensing the latter was more realistic.

Eric then let go of Moe's coat, and he practically jumped off the porch. "Hey, James!" Eric shouted. Moe turned briefly. "Don't forget what we talked about." Moe simply nodded and waved. Aqua and Ry followed closely behind him. By the time the boys got to the shortcut leading to Aqua's house, Moe had explained the whole bizarre incident and how glad he was that his friends had shown up when they did. Aqua explained that he meant to ask him before they ever left the library but forgot all about it until he was almost home. Ry just happened to be chatting with Aqua and didn't care to get home too soon.

The three boys were able to roll the pickup into the pole barn, thanks to a little ingenuity. With just the three boys pushing the vehicle on a slight incline, it may have been too much of a challenge for the trio, but Aqua hooked a come-along to a four-by-six-inch post on the back wall inside the pole barn, and though it was a slow process, it was an effective one. When they finished, Moe asked Aqua if he wanted to follow him home, hoping that Ry would take off toward his own house, because it was hard enough trying to work up the courage to tell Aqua about his journal, especially thinking it may have something to do with Supper's recent reclusiveness. He didn't want to include Ry just yet.

After rolling the barn door down when the truck cleared, the boys huddled next to the wood stove that Aqua's grandfather had been feeding all day so the building would be comfortable and dry to work in. His body could no longer take the cold, especially with the blood-thinning medication he was on. Henry was certain that it was the battery that needed to be replaced, which he'd had the foresight to buy several days before. When he got to the part of hoisting the old one out and putting the new one in, Aqua would need to be there to do the lifting.

"Dude, that is just some weird shit with your uncle," Ry said. Now that the chore was done, the boys could continue their conversation they'd had on the walk over.

"Yeah, that's just crazy," Aqua added. "You gotta keep away from that guy."

For the moment, Moe could only reply with, "Yeah, I know." Eventually, he knew, Ry would have to know too. In fact, all of his friends would, so why not tell the both of them now, then Creeper and Supper later? He contemplated his dilemma while Aqua and Ry dissected his uncle's behavior. Then, finally, Moe interrupted, "Hey, dudes, I got something that may have given my uncle reason to say the things he did."

"What do ya mean?" Aqua replied.

"I mean, I think my uncle may have found something that . . . gave . . . or . . . well, let him find out about the things we did."

"You mean the people on the river?" Ry asked, astonished.

"Yeah."

"I don't understand. How could your uncle know anything unless someone told him? Your ma didn't tell him, did she?" Aqua complained.

"Or wait, you said *found*. What could he have found? Nobody took pictures."

"Oh, dude, this doesn't sound good," Ry responded, slapping his hands to his cheeks.

Becoming agitated, Aqua persisted, "So that doesn't make any sense—how could he find anything out?"

"Yeah, bro, that doesn't make any sense at all," Ry added.

"I think he may have read this." Moe unzipped his coat, then the liner, and fumbled to grab his journal. When he pulled it out, his friends were confused at first.

"What is it?" Ry asked.

"Is that a diary?" Aqua muttered.

"It's not a diary, it's a journal."

"What's the difference?" Ry asked.

"It's for more serious thinking."

"What did you write in it?" Aqua asked. Moe's hesitation and reluctance to look up at his friends spoke volumes. "No! Oh my God! No! Tell me you didn't. What all did you put in there?"

By the time Moe looked up, there were tears in his eyes. "I'm sorry, bro."

Ry studied both of his friends, "Oh, shit! Oh, shit, oh, shit, oh, shit." Knocking his cap off, he tugged at his hair and hopped around. "Do you have all our names and stuff in there?"

Moe nodded, tears streaming down his face. He wiped his nose with his sleeve. "I'm sorry, man, I'm sorry! All right!"

When Aqua saw his closest friend crying, and genuinely regretful, it was difficult to condemn him, but it was also difficult not to be angry.

"Oh, shit, man, what are we going to do?" Ry demanded.

"Well, hold on, hold on," Aqua rationalized. "We're not completely sure that he read it yet, right?"

Moe shook his head, still sniveling, "I got a pretty strong feeling he did. It wasn't just the things he said, it was where I found the journal. It wasn't in the same place as I remember putting it. And also, the more I got to thinking about Sup, the more it made sense that I think my uncle told him and did something to him."

"Yeah, but none of us talked to him, dude," Ry nagged.

"I kinda agree with Moe. There's something very funny about Sup not calling, not coming to school, his quad being warm at the house. And plus, when we were watching him through the window that night, seeing him hugging his mom the way he did. I don't ever remember Sup hugging anybody. Do you?" Aqua asked, looking back and forth between his friends. "We gotta find out. We're going to have ta talk to Sup."

"Yeah, I think you're right," Moe agreed.

"What about Creeper?" Ry asked.

"We'll tell him tomorrow, right after school. Then we'll all go to Sup's house before his folks get home from work," Aqua explained.

"Do you think Sup will talk to us?" Ry asked, worried.

"We'll have to make him somehow," Aqua said confidently.

Moe felt better about Aqua's determination. His confidence and rational plan was also a motivation for Ry. After school the next day, the trio made up the excuse they couldn't get the pickup in the pole barn and needed an extra hand. Heading toward Aqua's house was roughly the same direction as heading toward Supper's. The boys wanted to get their friend as far away from other people as possible. Getting him on a path in the woods was a good place to tell him the news about Moe's journal and what his uncle may or may not know. In a quick burst of rage, Creeper asked Moe how he "… could be so fucking stupid," then hit him, but Moe was quick and a better scrapper. The punch landed on the left side of Moe's forehead, and through instinct and pain, Moe sprang back at Creeper and tackled him to the ground, flailing with a barrage of wild punches. Both Aqua and Ry broke up the fight, forcing Aqua to reason with Creeper and telling him they had few alternatives, and that what happened was over with, and all they could do now was work together to try to solve the problem. The reasoning spoken in cryptic flashpoints and using a fourteen-year-old's lexicon and experience still came across poignantly as the best course of action, the only course of action.

The boys made their way over to Tannery Road, which ran adjacent to the old railroad grade. None of them had a plan on how to coax Supper out of his house, or even on how to get him to open the door, so when they neared the home, they stood in the tree line like a small band of marauders studying a family of homesteaders before their attack. The house was a two-story with attached garage and a manufactured log built home. Four hundred feet from its walkout deck on the west side was Carr Lake, a twenty-plus acre body of water that was vaguely defined by swamps on the north, south, and southwest borders. On the east shore, where Supper's family and three other homes were built in the eighties, it had a unique population of birch clusters, giving the small lake a distinguished appearance, like a well-aged gentleman. For the boys, the lake wasn't good for much. With no beach, swinging tree, or privacy to go skinny-dipping, because all four homes could view the entire lake, it was a buzz kill. Plus, it wasn't even a very good bass lake. It had pan fish, but for the trouble, the boys would rather go to village park on the much larger Burton Lake and fish off the break wall at the mouth of the river. It did, however, make for a good skating pond during the winter, and that was provided the boys didn't make too much noise in their excitement. Because of the seclusion of the lake, sounds echoed, agitating two of the retired neighbors when the friends used foul language.

"You know, I bet he has to let Belle out once in a while," Ry said, referring to the family's black lab "Maybe we can stop him then."

"Yeah, but what if the dog picks up our scent first and gives us away? Sup could duck back in the house before we could get to him," Creeper suggested.

"Or maybe the dog will never need to go to the bathroom the whole time we're here," Moe added.

Without warning, Aqua ran toward the house in a crouched position. Moe shouted in a high whisper, "What are you doing?" but Aqua only turned briefly to give him the shush sign, then made his way up onto the front porch. The boys watched as Aqua slowly turned the knob to the front door of the house and cracked the door open. He flashed the other boys, still hiding in the woods, a look of surprise. Thinking his friends would remain where they were, Aqua cautiously stepped inside. Just when he made his way into the foyer, and before he could shut the door, Belle charged down the steps from the upstairs, barking. But when she recognized Aqua, she began wagging her tail.

"Mom, is that you?" Supper shouted from halfway down the staircase.

Aqua could see his legs but didn't answer. He reached down and scratched Belle's ears.

"Mom?" Supper asked again, then took two more steps so he could bend over and look through the railings toward the front door. When he saw Aqua standing there waving at him, he asked sharply, "What do you want?"

"I just wanted to see what you're up to, dude. You know, see how you're doing."

"I'm doing okay. But you're going to have to go, and you probably shouldn't just walk into people's houses uninvited."

"I knocked, but no one answered," Aqua lied, still scratching Belle's ears, with the dog now sitting at Aqua's feet.

Taking a couple more steps down the staircase so he could give Aqua a look of disbelief, Supper responded, "Well, you know we have a doorbell."

"Yeah, sorry, dude. I hadn't been here in a while. I didn't think of it . . ." Aqua knew he had to keep the conversation going. He had to try something. He also knew he had to get Supper closer. "We haven't seen you in school, and the guys and I were wondering if you were okay."

"I'm fine, and you can tell the others if you want that I'm probably not going to be back at school. Next week, we're moving to Wisconsin, so my parents took me out of school until I can start over there."

"Wow, dude, that sucks."

"Yeah, well."

"So can I get a drink of water before I walk back home?"

"Sure." Supper didn't move. Aqua walked over toward the kitchen, out of sight.

"Where do you keep the glasses again?" Aqua shouted.

Rolling his eyes, Supper walked the rest of the way down the steps and across the living room. From where the living room met the kitchen, Supper pointed to the cupboard above the countertop and by the stove. "Over there." Just as he did, Belle started barking again toward the front door. Both Supper and Aqua turned in surprise. The other three boys were on the porch, and Ry opened the door, with Moe and Creeper directly behind him. Supper was too stunned to move, especially when he made eye contact with Moe. Supper, pointing to the outside, yelled, "Get out of my house!"

Aqua walked toward Supper with his hands up, as if caught in a hostage negotiation. "Now, wait a minute, Sup. We all just wanted to talk to you."

"I want everyone out, now!" Then, pointing directly to Moe, he added, "Especially him!"

Aqua started walking closer to Supper. Noticing this, Supper sprang toward the staircase. Belle, thinking the boys were playing, possibly remembering the times when they were younger and chased one another around the yard, jumped up against Supper, accidentally knocking him to the floor. All the boys ran in, circling Supper, with Aqua passing him and standing at the foot of the stairs to block his exit. Supper stood up and shouted at all of them again to get out of his house.

"Look, dude, we think maybe Moe's uncle did something or said something to you," Aqua stated spontaneously.

Glaring at Moe, Supper snarled, "You fucking wrote about all of us! How could you do something like that?" He went from rage to tears in a matter of seconds.

"Look, I'm sorry, bro. Honestly, I didn't think anyone would ever find it or know. That was just something I wanted to keep to myself."

Supper sat on the coffee table, and, in a defeated voice, asked, "Can everyone just please leave?"

The other four boys looked around at each other for a signal on what to do next, but, eventually, everyone focused their attention on Aqua, while Belle was still going from boy to boy to see what game they were going to play next.

"Um, Sup . . . the guys and I were talking, and we think Moe's uncle did something to you and he may be trying to do some other things," Aqua spoke cautiously.

"Just leave," Supper begged and began to sob. He was defeated.

"We were thinking about doing something to him. You know, like getting rid of him," Ry announced, shifting his eyes around to his three standing friends.

There was a silence. Everyone waited for Supper to answer. Aqua wanted to add something, wanted to frame the suggestion in a different way, and no one expected Ry to say it first, but it was out there, and they all froze with anticipation.

Supper mumbled, "Do mean like get rid of him, get rid of him?"

"Yes," Aqua replied definitively. "Absolutely."

Supper looked up as if for an answer from the other boys as well, and they all nodded. Then Creeper affirmed it with, "We're all in."

CHAPTER 12

When Moe finally returned home, he had to use his key to get into the house. He was glad not to see Eric there, but his mother wasn't there, either. She was supposed to be off from work, since she was pulling the late shift because of some ladies taking off for opening day, so he was hoping to spend a little bit of time with her. At first, he became anxious, because he immediately thought his uncle might be doing something to his mother as well. Then he saw the note: "Took your uncle to shop for some clothes. Be back around seven. There's some leftover meatloaf and potatoes in the fridge. Love Mom."

It was closer to eight o'clock by the time Karen and Eric returned home. Eric walked in behind Karen with two large Kohl's bags. Moe noticed and knew immediately where they had been.

"Did you go all the way to Luce?" Moe asked, astonished.

"Yep," Karen replied, looking displeased and tired.

However, in contrast to her reply, Eric responded with noticeable pleasure. "We sure did there, Chief, and your uncle got himself some really cool duds. This calls for a big ole glass of orange juice."

Seeing his Uncle Eric's smug grin, and noticing his mother's expression, made getting rid of his uncle even more urgent. But he had to stick to the plan. Just one more night. He had to make it through the night. When Eric was in her bedroom, he approached his mother.

"Mom?"

"Yeah, hon?"

"Would you mind if I sleep in my room tonight?"

"Why, of course not. Besides, you should be up before I get home." She put her hands in his hair. "What's wrong, sweetie? You getting tired of that couch?"

"Yeah."

"Well, hopefully your uncle will be leaving soon, now that he's got his health back," Karen said in a quieter voice.

"Hey, why did you pick sleeping in my room instead of staying in your own and letting Uncle Eric stay in mine?"

"I guess I figured you'd know I wouldn't mess with your stuff and be more at ease with that."

Hearing that made Moe believe his uncle hadn't said anything yet to his mother about what he found. It was starting to make Moe lose his appetite. The proof of that was when Karen opened the fridge.

"What's wrong? Weren't you hungry? You didn't touch the meatloaf, and you love my meatloaf. You didn't stop after school and get a bite to eat with your friends, did you?"

"Yeah, I did," Moe lied. He knew she would offer to fix him something else instead of going to bed and getting some rest if she thought he hadn't eaten.

Karen gave Moe a disappointed look and said, "Well, I guess you can have meatloaf sandwiches for lunch tomorrow, then."

"Sounds good to me."

During the two hours Karen slept before getting ready to go to work, Eric didn't speak to his nephew, but, then again, Moe pretended to be doing homework at the kitchen table the whole time. He could, however, feel his uncle's glances and stares from the living room. After Karen woke up and started getting ready, Moe kissed his mother good night, told her to have a good night at work, then went into his room, and as soon as he heard her shut the front door, he delicately locked his bedroom door. If he slept at all that night, it was in half-hour stretches. At one point, while he was awake, he heard the doorknob being tested from the hallway. When morning came, he got ready in his room and stayed there until he heard his mother pull into the yard, for fear of running into his uncle without a buffer. By the time she arrived, he had to pee so desperately, he nearly urinated on himself before he could undo his pants once he got into the bathroom.

After school that day, the four boys met with Supper at the library, and he handed them a brown paper bag. Until his mother left for work on the eve of opening day for firearm deer season, the bulk of the plan was left in Moe's hands to execute.

When Moe returned home, Karen had just finished a load of laundry, the majority of which were Eric's new clothes. And when she asked Moe if he wanted to get dinner started, he asked her to wait a little longer. But then, it wasn't long after that, that Uncle Eric asked, in a very presumptuous way, when and what they were having for dinner. "I thought I'd fix burgers and fries tonight, if that's all right with everyone."

"Wow, meatloaf one night and hamburgers the next. Way to switch it up there, Sis."

"What an ungrateful asshole," Moe said under his breath, while standing next to his mother in the kitchen, as she started patting the meat.

Karen told Moe to hush but couldn't help snicker as soon as he said it. As Karen was setting the table, Moe was flipping the burgers.

"Does everyone want cheese on their burger?" Karen shouted.

"Yes, definitely," Eric yelled from the living room. "And I'll have two burgers, please."

Moe, who loved a good cheeseburger, decided not to have cheese on his that night because the ones he separated for his uncle, while his mother wasn't looking, got a special a white powder sprinkled on top before he put on the cheese. Then, when he poured the drinks, he made sure he shook up the half gallon container of orange juice before he poured a glass for his uncle. Karen seldom drank orange juice, and certainly never after breakfast. Uncle Eric took his dinner into the living room and ate off the tray he used while he was still in traction, so he could watch *American Idol*. Moe sat at the table with his mother. When they were finished, they went into the living room to watch the rest of *American Idol* with Eric. Moe was glad to see that he had eaten both burgers and drank all of the juice, but when Eric asked, "Hey, amigo, could you pour your uncle another glass of OJ?" Moe became a little worried that he was consuming too many drugs and would die in front of his mother.

"Ah . . . sure."

When Moe came back with only half a glass, Eric corrected him. "This isn't closing time at the bar. Give a full shot there, bartender."

So, Moe went back and topped off the glass. When the show was over, Karen told Moe she was going to get ready for work and that she needed to get there early that night because she was filling in for someone who kept a sloppy workstation. She also said she wanted to make sure it was squared away before she was on the clock, so her production wasn't compromised. Moe was happy to hear that because every time he looked over at his uncle, the man's eyelids were getting heavier and heavier. By the time Karen was finished in the bathroom and had grabbed her coat and purse from the bedroom, Eric was passed out on the couch, with his head tilted back, legs crossed, and hands folded across his lap. Moe was sitting in the recliner watching television and pretending not to notice.

"Wow! looks like your uncle had a little too much orange juice," Karen mused to her son.

"What? What do you mean?" Moe answered, trying to sound innocent, and mildly defensive as he thought maybe she suspected he had slipped him some drugs.

"I mean, he might as well have drunk a fifth of whiskey." Karen ruffled Moe's curly, disheveled hair playfully, then bent over and gave him a kiss on the cheek. That was something she didn't do much with Eric around. "You have a good night and leave a message for me at work if you decide not to go to school tomorrow."

"What?" Moe answered, somewhat distracted, while glancing over at his uncle to see if it looked like he was breathing.

"Remember, tomorrow is opening day. There probably won't be too many kids in school."

"Oh, yeah, yeah, right."

"I just don't know why they don't close the school. Around here, deer season is like Christmas. But what do I know?" Karen said sarcastically. She looked out the window of the front door and turned the porch light on. "Will you look at that crap, it's snowing again. The weather man said it was supposed to rain. I guess I better wear my boots. Who knows what it's going to do." Eric made a short snort in his sleep. "Well, as long as he doesn't start snoring, you should be able to enjoy watching television." Karen smiled at her son. "Have a good night, sweetie."

"You too, Mom."

Karen walked out the door. As soon as his mother backed out of the driveway, Moe called Supper's cell phone, which he had promised to keep with him.

"Hello?"

"Hey, dude."

"Yeah, is your uncle out already?"

"Oh, he's out, and my mother just left. But I think I may have given him too many drugs. I crushed up the Valium like you said and put it in his dinner."

"Did you crush up the oxycodone and put it in his drink?"

"Yeah, but it didn't look like much, so I crushed up some . . . I'm not sure what it is called for sure... I think vi-co-din. It's stuff my uncle had sitting on the shelf that he got when he got out of the hospital."

"Fuck, dude! You put that stuff in there too?"

"Yeah. And now I'm worried that he's gonna be dead before we get him out of the house."

"My dad said people don't normally die from pain killers and muscle relaxers, but they can go into like a comatose state or something. I'll get a hold of Creeper and pick him up on the quad, if you wanna call Aqua and Ry," Supper added with urgency.

"All right, dude."

Aqua got to the house first, with a five-gallon drywall bucket and a vinyl tarp rolled up inside, closely followed by Ry, then Supper and Creeper on the quad, pulling a sled that Supper's father meant to use for ice fishing, but never found the time. They all sneaked out of their houses in their own special way, like they had done many times before—through the window, out the back door, whatever they could do. Supper quietly pushes the ORV and sled out to the road before starting it. When Supper stepped through the doorway in Moe's house, behind Creeper, he was already unsteady. After the other boys put on surgical gloves provided by Supper, who had taken them from his mother's office, and started moving Eric around so they could handcuff, tie, and duct tape him, Supper stayed by the door. Aqua looked up and noticed this.

"Hey, Sup, what's wrong?"

Supper didn't answer. Keeping his hands in his pockets, he leaned back against the wall as if to steady himself. The other boys stopped and looked over at him. Aqua walked over, immediately sensing that something was wrong. He put his hand on Supper's arm. He could feel waves of tremors like someone who had been in the cold too long, shivering, then controlling it, then shivering again. But Aqua knew it wasn't from the cold.

"I don't know if I can do this," Supper said in a low, barely audible, shaky voice.

Aqua looked over at the others with concern. "That's all right. We'll get everything ready. We just may need some help lifting him onto the sled. Would that be, okay?" Aqua responded, keeping his voice as soothing as he could.

Supper nodded. The other four friends continued their chore, which it definitely was, none of them having realized how heavy the man was, but the struggle also gave them a sense of how powerful and domineering he could be if he were conscious. So, they hurried, with every moan that he made startling the boys and causing them to jump. After pushing the coffee table and ottoman aside, they laid out the six-by-ten tarp on the living room floor. Once they had Eric on the tarp, and before they could roll him over to lay prone, he sat partway up to try to prop himself on an elbow, but he was unsteady, weak, and delirious. The boys all froze. He mumbled something incoherently, vomited, and collapsed back to the floor.

"Ew," Ry complained, disgusted.

"That's okay," Aqua said. "He did it on the tarp."

The boys rolled him over on the tarp, so he was facedown. Creeper cuffed him with the cuffs he brought from home, they tied his ankles together, and duct tapped his mouth after gagging him with a dish rag.

"What if he throws up again and he can't spit it out? Will he drown in his own vomit?" Creeper asked.

"Well, if that happens, I guess he gets lucky, then," Aqua replied, smiling. The other boys chuckled, except for Supper.

Using the tarp as a sling, with all the boys except Supper grabbing a corner, they lifted and dragged the uncle out the door and onto the sled hitched to the quad. The sled was only five feet long, and Eric's feet hung off the back. Careful not to suffocate him, the boys wrapped the tarp loosely, but well enough that the body outline wouldn't be distinguishable to anyone who may pass by. Plus, they put the bucket over his feet, so that if anyone saw them, it would look as though they were hauling tent poles. As it was the evening before opening day, it wasn't uncommon to see other quads, with some late start hunters, especially from downstate, setting up camp at the last minute. Supper drove, with Creeper riding tandem, while the other boys rode precariously on the sled, prepared to wrestle Moe's uncle if he stirred, and careful not to put too much weight on top of him.

They followed an old skid trail through the woods behind Moe's house, then traveled behind a row of ranch and modular homes, cutting across the road through a vacant lot and onto the abandoned railroad bed. One mile south, they turned off onto a trail that few knew about, which led to the best spot to cast for steelhead on the river. They pulled up next to a bend in the river with several cedar trees, where the ground was mossy and spongy because of the dense root system. In fact, because of the root system, the bank jutted out over the current of the river four to five feet, like the brim of a hat. It was there that the boys lifted and dragged Eric till they had him right next to the ledge. A wet, heavy snow was still coming down, but under the canopy of the interwoven cedar branches and the high bank west of them, the boys were largely protected from the weather. The boys all put on their headlamps, then tied Eric's legs to the base of two trees five feet apart. From there, they needed to uncuff Eric, put his hands above his head, and simply tie his hands to a tree, so he'd be in the center of the triangle. However, the exposure to the outside, when he was only dressed in socks, sweats, and a T-shirt, may have caused his senses, previously numbed or dormant because of the opiates, to revive. At the moment, Eric was lying back on his arms, because his hands were cuffed behind him. He was starting to move, unfamiliar with the discomfort.

"Quick, we got to get his hands tied to the tree," Aqua demanded.

Creeper unlocked the cuffs, but when he did, Eric pulled his arms apart and started rocking his head back and forth. His eyes rolling, he tried to steady them. Tried to focus on one of the boys. All were scrambling to try to hold his arms. Only Supper was standing still, looking down at the big man in a frozen state. Even though he couldn't make Supper out from the glare of his light in his eyes, Supper felt as though he was looking through him. Eric tried speaking, tried shouting, but the gag prevented him. Aqua and Ry were fighting with one arm, while Moe and Creeper wrestled with the other, but Eric was becoming more powerful by the second.

"Sup, you got to help us, man!" Aqua cried as his voice changed pitch in mid-sentence.

In his left hand, Uncle Eric had Creeper by the collar and started twisting. Creeper began choking, but still fought. Moe had his knees in the vomit that was still in the tarp from earlier and kept slipping.

"Goddamn it, Supper! Fucking help!" Aqua demanded. Again, his voice oscillated.

Supper jumped on Eric's chest, pressing his knees into his shoulders. Eric loosened his grip on Creeper, and the boys were able to push his arms above his head and handcuff him again. Ry grabbed a rope and looped it between the cuffs, throwing both ends on either side of the tree. Aqua quickly grabbed one end and Moe the other, pulling Eric's arms above him. Then, Creeper and Ry joined them, pulling like tug-of-war, until they could tie the two ends around the tree. When they were finished, Moe's uncle was stretched like a snapshot of someone in the middle of making a snow angel. Eric was tied so tight that with his arms on either side of his head, he couldn't turn it. He could, however, raise it to look beneath him. Supper then jumped off him and stumbled back, landing on his butt and remaining there. All the boys watched the man while collecting their breath, mostly on their knees. Because of the adrenaline, Eric was alert, all of his senses heightened in fear.

"Okay," Aqua began. "We've got to get his clothes off him."

Aqua took his folding knife out of his pocket. First, he cut off Eric's T-shirt and pulled it out from underneath him. As planned, Ry got out the large Ziploc bag and Aqua stuffed the shirt in. Then he cut up the legs of the sweats. With this, Moe had to help pull them out from underneath him. And again, the boys stuffed the article of clothing in the plastic bag. Eric tried screaming, but it was a futile attempt through the washcloth and duct tape. Aside from the socks, which the boys couldn't remove because of the rope tied around the ankles, Eric now lay naked on the tarp.

"Is everybody ready for this?" Aqua asked. Lights flickered up and down as some nodded, and there were a couple of faint "yeahs." Taking a deep breath, Aqua said, "Ry, can you please fill the bucket?" Ry scooped a bucket of water from the river. "Okay, Sup, I think you should do this." Aqua turned around and looked at his friend.

"Yeah, Sup. It should be you, if any of us," Creeper agreed.

"Come on, dude, you can do it," added Ry.

Standing up, Sup stepped toward Aqua. "I don't know if I can do it, man."

"We know you can do it," Moe said. "Bro, that piece of shit needs to see you do it."

"Moe's right, it has to be you," Aqua added.

Supper stepped side by side to Aqua. Aqua handed him the knife. The two boys got down on their knees between Eric's legs. "Remember, dude," Aqua began reassuringly, "just the way I told you. You want to cut a diamond shape around the penis and balls." When Supper got the knife close to the flesh, his hand started to tremble. Trying to steady it with the other one didn't help. Aqua put a hand on top of Supper's to help steady them. Seeing this, Eric tried wiggling his body to resist. "Can someone sit on his chest, so he doesn't move as much?" Moe and Creeper both sat down on him. As soon as the boys started cutting through the skin, Eric started to pee. All the boys jumped back and off before they could get any on them. They stood back and watched as the man's bowels unloaded as well.

"Oh, fuck! He just shit and pissed himself," Ry announced disgustedly.

Aqua grabbed the bucket and started dumping it on Eric's crotch to flush the excrement and urine away. Eric was trembling from the ice-cold water. Then Aqua scooped up another bucketful and flushed the area again. Eric's body was a series of tremors. The boys all took to their positions again, Moe and Creeper on Eric's chest, and Aqua and Supper kneeling by his crotch. Supper continued to cut from the small wound he already created, but he was steadier now, so Aqua let go.

"That's it, you got it, dude," Aqua said with encouragement. "Just a little deeper."

"Man, that sure is a lot of blood," Supper noted.

"That's because he's still alive. Still pumping blood."

Eric's legs stiffened. There were muffled screams because of the gag, but they were forceful, veins rising on his forehead and temples, yet the boys were unaffected as Supper continued. He methodically pulled apart one side to cut through the sinewy tissue, tendons and veins, then the other side, until the penis and testicles were completely cut free from the body, and it was in Supper's hands. All the boys stood up. Aqua immediately grabbed the remaining half bucket of water and poured it over the opening in Eric's body. Eric raised his head, and his eyes bulged as he saw what they had done to him. He screamed hysterically, rolling and shaking his head uncontrollably, blood oozing out of him, following a crease in the tarp and down along the inside edge of his right leg and out onto the ground.

"Wow, that's gross looking," Ry said almost whimsically.

Supper walked over and held Eric's fleshy stump above his head. "There's your fucking cock, you bitch. What do you think of that? You got a big, red, ugly pussy now, don't you?" Supper clenched his teeth and knelt beside Eric, dangling the penis closer. "I think I'm going to shove this in your mouth. Or maybe I'll shove it up your ass first, then shove it in your mouth."

"Sup, you can't do that just yet," Aqua corrected. "If we pull his gag off, he could shout and draw attention. There might be a hunter out here somewhere, especially on the other side of the river."

"Then I'll just shove in his fucking face." Supper rubbed the bloodied appendage in Eric's face, smearing the blood from his hairline to the gag on his mouth. "How do you like that, bitch? Huh? Huh?" Supper started laughing uncontrollably, as if it were an allergic reaction.

"All right, Sup," Aqua said, concerned. "We gotta finish this up and get outta here."

"Yeah, bro. We're gonna get caught if we don't hurry," Moe agreed. "Besides, it looks like he's going to bleed to death before we can finish."

Supper complied almost begrudgingly, then tossed the genitals on the tarp and knelt down again with Aqua near Eric's bloodied crotch. This time, Moe and Creeper stood off to the side with Ry.

"Now you have to cut carefully around the anus," Aqua instructed. "Hey, who brought the string?"

"Oh, here ya go." Moe pulled the string out of his pocket and handed it to Aqua.

"Thanks, dude."

Eric flexed his butt cheeks together when Supper tried to guide in the knife to cut around the anus, making the task difficult, plus, all the blood was making the area hard to define.

"Shit, can someone help with this?" Aqua asked, looking up at the shadows with headlamps. Creeper stepped over the body with his back facing the river and squatted by Supper and Aqua.

"What do you want me to do?"

"Try and get your fingers in there." Aqua forced his hand under one of Eric's legs to demonstrate. "When you pull that butt cheek, I'll pull the other side here, and hopefully Sup can get the knife in there and cut around the hole."

The two boys pulled, and Supper worked meticulously but quickly to saw around the anus. More blood started spurting, and the task was becoming harder and harder to navigate. Supper was becoming sloppy and getting aggravated. He kept having to wipe the blood away to see where he was cutting. But Eric started to weaken, losing large puddles of blood on the tarp. At one point, the boys had to back away and let Ry and Moe douse the area with river water. Once the rectum was finally detached, Aqua held onto the knife and handed Supper the string. Supper tied the rectum off, just as Aqua was taught by his grandfather with the buck he'd shot. Aqua handed back the knife, then Supper carefully took the knife and, in the opening above the genitals, with the blade facing up, and being careful not to slice the intestines or organs, slowly cut and sawed a vertical line up Eric's body to just below the sternum, after carving around one side of the belly button. Eric's eyes started to flutter, and Ry noticed.

"I think we're losing him, dudes," warned Ry.

"Quick, get some more water!" Aqua shouted.

Ry scooped up another three or four gallons and handed it to Aqua. Aqua poured it over the abdomen that was spreading open on its own, then poured the rest over Eric's face. Eric tilted his head up and looked back down at his stomach in time to see his intestines rising above the surface of his skin. He tried to scream again and feebly started to try to free himself again, but the more he fought, the more his skin spread apart. The boys watched a little longer, until Eric went into hemorrhagic shock. At this point, Supper discarded the smaller rubber gloves he had on, putting them into one of the Ziploc bags, then he put on some longer cleaning gloves that went up to his elbows. He then lifted and pulled the intestines and organs from the body cavity and rolled them over to Eric's side and onto the tarp. The heart stopped during the process. Pausing for a few seconds to shine his headlamp on Eric's face, with the eyelids held ajar and the corneas rolled back, Sup got the affirmation needed that the man was no longer a threat. Supper continued to cut more tissue, tendons, veins, and arteries, and at the last, severed the esophagus and trachea. The boys pulled the body over to the side on the mossy ground. They lifted the corners of the tarp and spilled the contents into the river. Entrails hooked onto some cedar roots jutting out over the water, unraveling the intestines and organs that got caught in the current. Aqua took a stick and unhooked them. Some would sink, some would float, but most of it would be eaten by fish, turtles, crayfish, otters, raccoons, and seagulls.

"Man, that guy took a long time to die," Creeper observed with the same admiration he had for the physical prowess of Harry Houdini and the length of time he could hold his breath or hang upside down in shackles and work himself free.

Letting out a sigh of relief, Ry added, "Fuck, I thought he'd be dead after his dick was cut off."

The boys flushed out the body, rinsed off the tarp, wrapped it back up, and lifted it back onto the sled. Before they left, Supper took a pack of menthols out of his inside coat pocket. They were from one of his mother's many forgotten hiding places. Supper lit a cigarette, and the boys took turns burning another dot on one another's back; re-lighting the smashed tip as needed. Maybe it was the cold, adrenaline, or simply a numbness that came over them, but the burn was hardly felt by any of the boys. There was no preparation or psyching oneself up this time. As they pulled away from the riverbank, Aqua regretfully and painfully threw the knife his grandfather had rewarded him with, into the rapid river. *What will I tell Pa if he ever asks?* Aqua thought.

On the ride back, they rode along the railroad bed and stayed on it until they came up just shy of the businesses in town. The wind shifted and was coming out of the southwest. The temperature climbed, gradually turning the snow to rain, creating a fog. Supper shut down his quad and, after unhitching the sled, the boys pushed the four-wheeler down a ditch and into a large culvert designed for spring runoff. All the boys then pulled the sled the rest of the way until they came up behind the barbershop and Pat and Joe's apartment. While Ry kept lookout to see if anyone stirred in the apartment or any lights came on, the other boys lifted the tarp-wrapped body onto their shoulders and ran it across the road, staying in the trees between the entrance to the state park and the parking lot where the buck poles were staged for sun up and opening day of deer season. They then waited for the signal from Ry, who was standing on the tin roof of the fish smokehouse across the street and behind the branches of a huge white pine that spread out over the top of it. From this vantage point, he could see both up the hill leading south out of town and north toward the other businesses and bridge by the library. But he really could see very little, as the fog was getting denser. There were pulleys with hooks already in place on the top of the buck poles. Aqua found some nylon rope lying behind the Bait Pile, which he used to have something to connect the hook to, coiling it several times around the neck. The friends hoisted the body twelve feet into the air until the pulley could go no farther. Then they tied it off and ran back into the tree line, across the road, then, grabbing the sled, they pulled it back to the quad, hitched up, and headed home. It was two thirty in the morning.

By the time Aqua got home, it was raining so hard that the tin on the pole barn roof rang like machine gun fire. The pole barn stove was still burning pretty strong. His grandpa always liked to keep it warm. Aqua warmed himself for a moment, then threw in Moe's vomit-soiled pants, the Ziploc bags, the tarp, a few never-worn clothes from Kohl's, a man's pair of shoes, and just when he was about to throw in the journal, as he'd promised his friends, Aqua stopped, read the first several pages, and smiled. Between the shelving his grandpa made for his power tools and the tin siding, there was a gap made by the horizontal two-by-fours. A perfect place for hiding things, and Aqua did. In the clouded night sky, rain, and branches of red and white pines, no one could see the black smoke coming from the chimney of the pole barn. When he was finished, Aqua ran through the rain, over behind the house outside his bedroom window, stepped up on the cinder block, slid the unlatched window pane up, and climbed in. He put on dry pajamas and hung his wet clothes in the closet to deal with the following day, before his grandpa found them.

When Pat Bachelder woke up at four thirty opening day, she walked over to the kitchen sink like she did every morning to look out over at her and her husband's restaurant across the street. It was a subtle reassurance, but subtle enough to give her the confidence to start another day of meeting new customers and sharing stories with the old ones. She genuinely liked people, and it was always less a business for her than it was a lifestyle. The streetlight usually illuminated the parking lot pretty well, but because of the heavy rain, fog, and the shadows cast by the other buck poles in front of it, she couldn't make out the carcass hanging in the rear.

"Joe!" Pat yelled.

"What?" Joe shouted back from the bathroom.

"Come out here. It looks like somebody already hung a deer."

"What?" Joe shuffled out of the bathroom in his slippers, scratching his large belly under his pajamas. He squinted out the window to see if he could make out the size of the deer. "Whatever idiot put that up there is probably going to lose his hunting license is all I can say. Shooting before sun up. But from here, at least it looks like a pretty good size buck. Can't make out any horns, though. I don't know how in the hell anyone can hunt in this kind of weather anyway." He turned toward the door, grabbing his raincoat and putting on his boots.

"Hold on. I'm coming with you," Pat insisted, grabbing her coat and boots as well.

Because the rain was pouring too hard to look up unnecessarily, it wasn't until the couple crossed the road that they noticed there was something strange about the shadowy figure twisting in the air. They held hands to steady themselves, and looking down, watched their steps, being careful not to slip in the rain and snow mix. Not until they were practically next to the figure did, they discover that it was a man, gutted and hollowed out, hanging by the neck on a hook, with a penis dangling from his mouth. Pat screamed manically, then, passing out, fell backward against the freezer that housed bags of Polar Ice to sell to patrons. Joe stumbled, trying clumsily to help his wife to her feet, but unconscious, she was dead weight. He couldn't hold his footing because of the slush and slipped to his knees.

"Help!" Joe cried. "Help, please! Someone help!"

When Karen returned home from her shift, she had already heard of a body found at the Bait Pile, but there were no details. The crew, while they were on a break, speculated that someone had hanged himself. Another rumor was that someone had pulled a prank. And yet another coworker heard that there was some sort of freakish hunting accident. Karen climbed in bed next to her sleeping child, laid up against him, and gave him a hug; he stirred a little, then she kissed the back of his head through his unruly hair.

"Hi, Mom," Moe mumbled, half asleep. "How was work?"

"Oh, work's work, that's all it is," she replied. "How did you and your uncle get along last night?"

Moe shrugged his shoulders effortlessly. "I dunno. I think somebody picked him up while I was in my room. I could hear some voices, but I wasn't quite awake, so I didn't pay much attention. I just remember hearing the front door shut."

"That's strange," Karen said aloud, but then thought to herself how she didn't know he knew anyone in the area, or, her worst fear, that one of his friends from Detroit had come up to visit. Then she thought maybe he met someone the other night when he borrowed her car. "Is he here now?"

"I couldn't tell ya." Moe yawned, his tired words seeming to stretch and oscillate. "I slept most of the night. Didn't hear anything until you just came in."

"Huh. Well, I hope you don't mind if your mother lies here with you for a little bit. I'm really beat." Karen yawned. She was worried about someone else her brother knew coming into her home but was too tired to dwell on it at the moment.

"That's okay. I like it when you lie down with me sometimes. It makes me feel safe."

"The fate of your planet rests not in the hands of gods. It rests in the hands of mortals."

– Thor (*Thor: Heaven & Earth #2*)